Preface

"A well-regulated militia being necessary
to the security of a free State, the right of the
people to keep and bear arms shall not be infringed."

Second Amendment, U.S. Constitution

Fiction and nonfiction are often times blurred.

My girlfriend of five weeks, Tabitha (T) and I were driving back to California after a great weekend at Lake Mohave with friends. It was our first trip together as a couple which was a huge test for our short pairing at the time. I'm not sure we were calling it a relationship yet. It was a huge test for T, since I was the last of our group of boys to get married, and a big test of our relationship since they had all kinds of "dirt" on me that she might not have been prepared for or want to hear just yet. Then there were the obvious things like, what does she look like in a bikini, can she drink, and how does she get along with the other wives?

As the trip ended and we started the four-hour desert drive back to reality, just staring at the same desert scene, frame after frame, an awkward silence fell over the cab of the truck. It caught me off guard, because T and I usually didn't have any problem filling up conversational space.

"What was this undercover assignment you worked?" T asked.

Ahh, now it made sense. I knew the source of this silence now. My friends must have told her after a few too many beers last night that

I'd worked a deep cover assignment and they'd lost contact with me for three years.

I quickly changed the subject, but she persisted for the next sixty minutes asking me question after question.

"What did you do? Did you have long hair? Did you do drugs? Did you kill someone?" she persisted.

"T, I will make you a deal. On our tenth wedding anniversary I will tell you everything you want to know, but until then, don't ask," I replied with a smile.

"Did you just ask me to marry you?" she quickly shot back.

"You wish…"

April 27, 2002

T and I were married in front of one-hundred-and-twenty-five of our closest friends and family members. After a beautiful ceremony and reception, we were traveling to our hotel room before leaving on a cruise for our honeymoon.

"You know Drew, the clock has officially started," T said as her eyes began to widen with her smile. T has the most beautiful big blue eyes I've ever seen.

"What clock is that?"

"You promised me that on our ten-year wedding anniversary you would spill the beans."

I just laughed because she said it like she knew all along she was going to marry me and was anticipating this conversation happening in ten years.

April 26, 2012

My wife and I climbed into the car to get on the road traveling to Big Sur, California to celebrate our ten-year wedding anniversary. I had planned a special getaway. We were staying at a beautiful little cottage along the coast of the ocean and I had planned hikes, massages, and great dinners. We were kid-free and looking for a little bonding time away from the chaos of life. After we stopped for lunch about half-way into our drive, the wine was beginning to flow and our bellies were full, T said, "Spill it."

As usual, even after ten years of marriage, I didn't have any idea what my wife was talking about.

"It's our ten-year wedding anniversary, so give me the scoop," she said.

I was caught off guard because she hadn't mentioned my undercover work for years and neither had I, but after all these years she still wanted answers.

Over the next few days, we talked about my undercover assignment and I answered question after question after question. I told her everything that I could remember: my experiences, my fears, my failures, things I was proud of and things that I was not proud of, my struggles, and my successes.

I had never reflected on those three years prior to this outing with my wife. I never realized how fascinating this assignment must be to an outsider, how it shaped me as a person, and how it would shape the rest of my life.

You should write a book someday…

A Bird is Born

"It is not the function of our Government
to keep the citizens from falling into error; it is the
function of the citizen to keep the Government
from falling into error."

Robert H. Jackson

Ted and Gina MacGregor's second child was born in July 1970: a premature boy came out screaming and full of fight, but had to stay in the hospital for three weeks before the doctors would let the MacGregors take him home. According to Gina, Little MacGregor cried for the first two years of his life and then never again. They were a family of four, living modestly in the suburbs about an hour outside of Los Angeles. Cindy, his sister, three years his elder, was close to her brother, and they never really got into the squabbles most siblings do.

Little MacGregor was vertically challenged throughout his childhood. The smallest kid on his sports teams and amongst his classmates, quickly little MacGregor acquired nick names such as Pee Wee, Munchkin, and Little Mac. He had a strong network of long-term friends and was above average athletically despite the challenge of his size, but never achieved legendary status in anything. Academics came quite easily to him throughout high school, but in college he met his match.

MacGregor's baby face, coupled with his vertical size challenge always made him look significantly younger than he really was. Soft spoken, shy, introverted, stubborn, determined, and a "rules" kid is how most would have described him. He was never the leader, but always belonged to the outskirts of the popular groups. He was talented enough to make all the varsity teams, but was never the star player. Throughout high school, he chased all the popular hot girls but he seemed to fall into the little brother category often, until his junior year when he found a hot-outskirt cheerleader who stole his heart and remained his companion throughout the rest of high school.

After high school, MacGregor was a boy with big dreams wanting to become a doctor to fulfill his father's wishes. Entering medical school, still a boy, not prepared for medical school's demands, he found himself academically subject to dismissal after his first year. Three years later, consumed in med school, he switched majors and his determination wouldn't allow him to fail. Graduating with a double major, but falling short of his dream to be a doctor, he found himself like most twenty-year-olds, not knowing the path for his life. As many medical student drop-outs do, MacGregor stumbled across the law enforcement profession and he fell in love.

After graduation from college, he pursued his new law enforcement dreams and started applying to several different police departments to no avail. Most departments weren't hiring in MacGregor's demographic, so he made a rash decision and quit his job as District Loss Prevention Manager in July of 1993 and put himself through the Sheriff's Academy with a long shot attempt to be more marketable. Told by his father all of his life to not have blind faith but to make his own luck, he graduated first in his class, in late 1993, yet wasn't offered a job with any law enforcement departments. He figured his skin was the wrong color – reverse discrimination, he thought. Broke and unemployed, he was forced to slum it with one of his good friends, Scooter, who was recently married and had just purchased his first home with his new bride, offering Mac a place to stay rent-free. Humbled, and at first reluctant, he accepted the offer and pressed on. His plan and aspirations of graduating No. 1 in the Sheriff's Academy bearing no fruit in the job market, he crawled back to his old boss and begged for his job back.

One night at Scooter's house, he was down and feeling frustrated. He was back at his old job and it didn't look like there was any hope in sight for him getting hired as a police officer. He could hear his dad's words echoing through his head – "I told you so, and no son of mine will be a cop" – and felt he'd truly hit a low point in his life.

He went for a walk, and found himself accompanied by Scooter.

"What are you doing? Go back to your guests, I'm just having a pity party for myself, I'm fine," said Mac.

"Ahh, I really don't like them much. I'd rather drink to your pity party, just don't tell my wife," Scooter chuckled.

"I'm done with this cop thing; my dad was right. I gave up everything and I worked my ass off. I graduated No. 1 in my class and I still can't get a job because I'm white and don't have a pair of tits! Screw it, I'll think of something else." Mac's pity party continued.

"Mac, as long as I've known you, you have never quit anything. You are one of the most tenacious guys I know. After all, let's face it. You are five-foot nothin' and you wrestled ninety-eight-pounds as a senior in high school! I've never seen anything stop you and I've definitely never seen you quit anything. Don't puss out now. Now let's go back and grab another beer and see if we can get you a pair of tits," Scooter said as he downed his Bud Light.

January 1994

MacGregor's hard work and sacrifice eventually paid off and he was offered two law enforcement jobs. The first was to join the Sheriff's Office as a deputy sheriff and the second was with the Los Angeles Police Department. He was excited to start his career in law enforcement but little did he know what his career had in store for him. He accepted the LAPD's offer and started the police academy in February. He graduated later that year, once again coming top of his class, and was assigned to a patrol division in East Los Angeles.

The Offer to Fly

"Let no guilty man escape,
if it can be avoided… No personal considerations
should stand in the way of performing a duty."

Ulysses S. Grant

October 1994

I looked into the mirror and straightened my crooked tie bar. I was dressed in my class A's, my shoes were polished, my gear was shined and my gun was oiled. I walked upstairs for my first roll call as a Los Angeles Police Officer in the East Los Angeles area. A skinny twenty-four-year-old kid, 6 feet, 155 lbs., shaved brown hair with hazel eyes, naïve to the ways of the world and cruelty of life. I could feel my heart beating against my bulletproof vest. My hands were sweating slightly and I felt a little sick from excitement.

Sitting in the front row that night, I was so excited, scared, and proud that I had finally made it. Over the next few months, I had the best time of my life and I never wanted to go home from work. I loved the thrill, power, and self-satisfaction that we helped people every day and as cliché as it may sound, put bad people in jail.

One morning after getting home from work, there were two messages on my answering machine at home: one from a detective asking me to give him a call and a second from a sergeant. As a young policeman, I was scared, thinking I had seriously screwed something up.

I called the detective first and he advised me about a court date on a 211 case.

The second phone call I made would forever change my life. I wrote down the name of the sergeant on the palm of my hand and dialed the phone number.

"Hello," a male voice answered. I quickly hung up the phone because I thought I'd misdialed. I listened to the message again and quickly dialed the phone number again to make sure I didn't forget it.

"Hello," the same male voice answered.

"I'm not sure that I have the right number, but I'm looking for a Sgt. Torres," I said.

"What makes you think that you have the wrong number, Drew?" the male voice answered again.

Silence… I was still processing the phone call.

"Did you just hang up on me, Drew?" the male voice continued. "This is Officer Drew MacGregor isn't it?" he asked again.

"Yes, sir, is this Sgt. Torres?" I finally responded.

"Yes, it is. I work for the Anti-Terrorist Division and I want to talk to you about an opportunity that you might have but I don't want to talk to you over the phone about it. Can you meet me tomorrow at the academy, near the picnic tables at 0800 hours?" Sgt. Torres said in a matter-of-fact voice.

"Sir?" came my involuntary response.

"Yes?" Sgt. Torres shot back like a game show host.

"May I ask what this is regarding?" I asked, thinking I was somehow in trouble.

"Yes, tomorrow you can ask me whatever you want," Sgt. Torres reiterated.

"Sir, we can't discuss it now?"

"What did I say, Junior? I said, I will answer all of your questions tomorrow in person," Sgt. Torres's voice hardened in response as he continued. "If you are interested, I will see you there."

"Okay, sir, thank you," I answered before Sgt. Torres cut me off.

"Drew? One last thing. Please don't tell anyone that I called you. I'll explain why in the morning."

"Okay, see you tomorrow sir," I answered as Sgt. Torres hung up.

After the phone call, I tried to get some sleep but couldn't; I'm not sure if it was from the sun coming through my window, my dog Justice wanting to play, or my mind trying to figure out what trouble tomorrow would bring.

Tomorrow

The sun woke up just as people oblivious to the atrocities that had occurred in the City of Los Angeles while they were sleeping began to rise. I drove up to the Los Angeles police academy after my shift and I remembered being exhausted as the last bit of adrenaline left my body from that night's patrol. I parked and walked up to the picnic tables located just south of the track. I was sitting on one of the picnic tables looking all around with a strange feeling in the bottom of my stomach. The only people I could see were the new police recruits running around the academy grounds, playing the game, like I had done a couple of months prior.

Two men approached me from the west. The first guy was about fifty years of age, a male Hispanic, salt and pepper hair, medium length, maybe 5'8, and 190 pounds, wearing a polo shirt and some slacks. He looked like a bad version of Santa Claus. The second guy was about forty-five, also male Hispanic, dark hair slicked back, with a full beard,

17

about 5'10, 210 pounds, wearing jeans, cowboy boots, and a shirt. He looked like a pudgy Mexican guy who ran a gardening business. I didn't see any badge, gun or police insignia. Quickly profiling these two men, they sure didn't look like police officers or top-secret undercover operatives to me; but I wasn't sure what to expect.

As the two men walked up one said, "Hi Drew, have you been waiting long?"

I was thinking, who the hell are these guys? But I went along with it. The older guy introduced himself as Sgt. John Torres (JT) and the second as Detective Jack Garcia. I decided I wasn't going to say much, just listen and find out as much as possible. Sgt. Torres started off with some bad jokes and small talk that I obliged with a courteous laugh, trying to figure out where he was coming from.

JT said, "I bet you're wondering who we are and what this is about?"

"Yes, sir," I replied.

I wasn't sure if I should ask them for their police identification or not; puzzled, I just kept quiet.

"Junior, we work for the Anti-Terrorist Division and I want to offer you a chance to become a UC in one of the most elite UC programs in the world," JT said. "Our UC program is the deepest undercover program of any law enforcement agency in the country. Our *birds* – which is what we call our undercover officers – go everywhere and have infiltrated the most impenetrable groups in the nation. Most officers and even the LAPD Command Staff don't even know this program exists and we want you to become one of us." JT stopped his sales pitch and waited for my response.

"You want me to become an undercover officer for the Anti-Terrorist Division? I don't know anything about terrorists or being an undercover officer," I replied with a nervous laugh.

JT continued, "You come highly recommended and we've been watching you and we think you'll make a great bird."

Perplexed, I said, "I was recommended and you've been watching me?"

"That's right, Drew! We've been watching you, that's what we do, and that's what you will do if you choose to join us," the pudgy guy, Jack, chimed in.

JT went on to tell me that their undercovers went everywhere, out of state and even international. He said that the selection process was long and vigorous, but before they went any further he needed to know my interest level.

"Who recommended me?" I asked.

The pudgy guy Jack chimed in quickly again in a stern voice: "Everything in this program is on a need and right to know basis… and right now you don't have either." I couldn't help but ponder if this guy had some mommy issues to explain his asshole disposition.

Ignoring pudgy Jack's response, I reframed my question as a more open-ended one: "Okay, what can you tell me?"

JT lowered his voice but the intensity in his tone increased. "What I'm about to tell you, you can't repeat to anyone. Do you understand?"

I remained silent, very intrigued, forgetting to provide an answer to his question.

"Do you understand, Drew?" JT's voice rose.

"Yes, sir," I answered.

JT appeared to relax, just slightly. "The program works like this. We ask for a two-year commitment once you are trained. Most birds are in training for about six months. You will take on another person's identity and live the next three years as that person. You will not be

Officer MacGregor anymore. You won't even be Drew MacGregor. You won't see Scooter or any of your friends; you will forget who you are for the next three years. Your girlfriend will be gone; your friends, mom, dad, sister, nobody will know your new identity, what you are doing or where you are at. Do you follow me, Junior?"

I started to laugh nervously, but didn't answer or acknowledge him.

JT continued, "You will live in an apartment somewhere in the city and you will have to go get another job, where you will go to work every day just like every other schmuck. You won't have a badge, gun, police identification. The only identification that you will carry will be for your new identity. The only friends or family that you will be allowed to talk to will be the new ones you make in your new life. You will live off of the money you make from your new job and your police salary will be saved for you, but you won't have access to it. Your money will be saved in a separate account under your name waiting for you when you get out. Are you still with me, Junior?"

I nodded, but I still wasn't sure if what he was telling me was real.

"Do you have any questions for me so far?" JT asked.

"What will my name be?" I asked. Realizing quickly; why would I ask that? Out of all the things JT just told me, my first and only question was what my name would be?

JT chuckled. "You have a long time before we get to that. You have to be accepted into the program first, Junior."

"What will I be doing or what terrorist group could I infiltrate?" I asked.

"Again, Drew, you may have the *need to know* that info, but you don't have the *right to know* that information yet. In due time, Junior, but basically you will be tasked with infiltrating a terrorist organization and collecting information on that group to see if they are a threat to the citizens of Los Angeles," JT explained.

"What terrorist organization can I infiltrate? Look at me," I responded with a smirk across my face.

"Drew, a terrorist could be anyone who 'Plans, threatens, or attempts to perform a significant disruption of public order' – it's not like the movies. You don't need to be an Arab with a towel wrapped around your head to be a terrorist," Pudgy Jack answered with a silent *idiot* implied at the end of his response.

"Okay, if you say so. But I'm just not seeing it. Look at me…
I'm a skinny pretty boy who's led a pretty sheltered life. I don't know
shit about guns, bombs, drugs; I've never been in the military and I don't
even know where Iraq or Iran is at."

JT laughed hard. "You think all terrorists come from Iraq or Iran?
Trust me, Junior, don't worry about that. I think you can do it or I
wouldn't be here. You just need to decide if you want to go through the
training. Training will tell us if you are cut out for the program or not."

"Okay…" I responded.

"What's going through your head? I can tell you have a ton of
questions. What are you thinking?" JT probed.

"I'm just processing what you said; you want me to give up my
life for three years, dump my girlfriend, not talk to my friends, family,
and give up the one thing I love and have worked so hard to become the
last two years, being a police officer. All of that, to go hang out with a
terrorist group I don't even know the name of and I would imagine they
wouldn't be too happy with me if they found out I was really a cop. Not
to mention, live in the ghetto, all while flipping burgers at McDonalds,"
I sarcastically summarized.

"Jack, do you hear this kid? I told you so, he's sharp!" JT slapped Jack on the shoulder. "Doesn't that shit sound exciting to you, Drew? Think of the ass James Bond got…" JT chuckled again.

"No, not really," I said, changing my tone. "Why would I do that? Are there any positives to this besides the company line of I'm protecting the citizens?"

"You would be one of the elite, the chosen few to work the program. You will be legendary and the Department takes care of their birds." JT winked at me.

"What does that mean?"

"One of the main perks outside of the career benefits is you will exit the program with a boatload of money!" JT said.

"What do you mean?" I asked again.

Jack chimed in this time. "Well, think about it. You'll get a second job or cover job under your new identity, right? You live off of that money for the next three years. You still get your full police salary that just gets banked into a separate secret account at the police academy. How much did you get hired on at?"

"I think about $32K with my degree."

"Well, do the math. That's $100K saved when you get out. That kind of money at your age is a life-changer, Junior. You could even buy a house."

JT continued, "Other perks are promotional opportunities. You will finish your probation while undercover and you will be eligible for all promotions – generally all birds come out of the program with a promotion. As I told you already, Drew, the Department takes care of its birds."

JT and Jack went on to tell me that completing the program would greatly enhance my career and that the top brass of the Department would take any bird that came out of the program and give them their choice of assignment. I would be one of the elite, the chosen few to have worked the program and it was a great honor and experience that very few could say they had done. JT and Jack ended the meeting by telling me to call them one week from today at exactly 0900 hours to let them know my decision. "You are not to tell anyone about this meeting or what we have discussed; not your family, friends, or your training officer," they reiterated.

I left the meeting just blown away. My first reaction was: *undercover, wow, 007, James Bond, the movies, how exciting, I'm in.*

Then as I started to think about it, I wasn't sure, there were a lot of things to consider. The biggest selling point to me was the financial part, because I was seriously in debt from putting myself through the Sheriff's Academy and college. My mind began to race as I made a pros and cons list in my head. All of my immediate family was out of state, and I really didn't see them much anyway. Most of my friends were moving on with their lives: Gary was doing the pilot thing; Scooter was married. But what about my girlfriend, Liz, and my dog, Justice? Those were tough ones. On the pro side, I could get out of debt and have enough money to buy a house when I got out. My career would be set by the time I got out, if what JT had said was true.

I couldn't stop thinking about it for the next week. It didn't matter what I was doing. After about three days had passed, I still hadn't decided what I was going to do, so I confided in Gary, breaking a rule, to get his opinion. We were driving to meet his family for dinner and I had told him about my job offer. At first Gary didn't believe me, because we often played practical jokes on each other. But soon Gary knew I was serious, due to the look on my face. He knew me better than anyone. He was just as blown away as I was… When I asked him what he would do in my situation he said, "I don't know, that's a tough decision."

We talked about it most of the night, the pros and cons. The next morning Gary walked into my room and said, "I would do it," then walked out to make our breakfast, strawberry crepes. In hindsight, I guess that was all I needed to hear, just someone else's validation that I was not crazy for accepting this assignment.

I called JT twice to ask him some administrative questions I had about the program during that crucial week. JT answered my questions with no further inquiry about which way I was leaning. On the decision day – a Monday – I was to call him at exactly 0900 hours. I was sitting on our couch, exhausted, trying to stay awake, because I had worked all night long. Finally, 0900 came around and I dialed the number.

Ring, ring, ring, ring… then a voice yelled, "JT's tamales."

Caught off guard, I paused and said, "Is JT there?"

"Speaking," he answered.

"This is Drew; I want to do it. I'm in, what's next?" I told him with a deep sigh.

"Are you sure? Do you need more time, because once you tell me yes there is no going back and it will change your life forever."

"Yes, sir, I'm sure. I'm in. What do I do now?" I answered after a short hesitation.

"Great! I'll call you in a couple of days and let you know what's next," JT said, hanging up.

Natural Selection

"For many are called, but few are chosen"

Mathew 22:14

The following week Jack contacted me at home. He stated that he was going to send me some paperwork for me to fill out through the inter-mail system and to call him or JT at the office once I had it filled out. A couple of days later I received the background at roll call, which was kind of strange. I was sitting in the front row – all boots or rookies sat in the front row at roll call – when my sergeant said, "MacGregor? Is there a MacGregor here?"

"Here sir," I said, raising my hand.

"Seriously, MacGregor! No wonder I had no idea who the fuck you were; you're just a boot! Why the hell are you getting mail? You have two seconds on the job and you're getting mail at my roll call? It better not happen again. Is that understood, MacGregor!" the shift sergeant yelled.

"Yes sir, it won't happen again," I answered back with a crackling voice as a few crumpled-up pieces of paper hit me in the back of my head, thrown from the back rows. I didn't dare turn around or say anything.

After roll call, I rushed down to the kit room so I could be first in line to retrieve our equipment for the night. The kit room door opened up.

"MacGregor and Rivas working 4A12 tonight, sir," I quickly muttered. "Can I get three radios, a shot gun, Taser, and a bean bag."

"MacGregor, you're assigned to Rivas? Good luck with that! Your shop number is 80016 and it's parked in the corner."

"Thanks!" I said as I ran off, trying to carry everything, find our car, get it gassed up, and make sure that the windows were washed all before Rivas came outside.

As Rivas walked out to start our shift, I was waiting in the car like I was supposed to do. He got in and we sat in silence. I knew his routine. I wasn't supposed to log on to the computer until he went to Tams to get his cheeseburger and coffee for the night. As we pulled out of the station he uncharacteristically pulled to the curb.

"Junior, why the fuck are you getting mail?" he yelled. "You're a boot – abide by the rules and play the game, knock that shit off, the guys will think you are *salty*, so don't embarrass me again!"

"Yes sir, it won't happen again." I was a little scared because I wanted to tell him the reason, but under strict orders not to by JT, I didn't. Rivas was a tough, seasoned guy who had spent his entire career on the streets, and he looked like he would, or wanted to, kill you, all the time.

After my EOW (end of watch), I went straight home and filled out all the paperwork, which included a more in-depth background from what had been required to get on the job. As soon as the paperwork was filled out, I proofread it to make sure every box was filled out, the information was accurate, and it was spelled correctly.

I called JT that night. "Sir, I have the paperwork for you."

"Keep it with you and I'll get it from you later," he said.

"Sir, I have it completed. Do you want me to send it to you?" I asked.

"Junior, what did I just say!" he barked.

"Okay, I just thought…"

JT stopped me, yelling, "If I wanted you to think I would have told you to think. Everything I tell you to do has a purpose, but you seem to think you know more than me. Just keep your mouth shut and do what I tell you."

I hung up the phone defeated, wondering what the heck this guy's problem was. I was trying to give him my packet because I was excited and he'd asked for it.

Ten days had gone by and I hadn't heard anything from JT or from Pudgy Jack. I was getting a little antsy, but I wasn't about to call JT again seeing how our last phone call had ended. It was a Tuesday, my Friday at the time, and my girlfriend Liz and I went out to eat at her favorite restaurant, Don *Jose*'s, just as we did every Tuesday night. When we arrived, we were seated at our usual table and ordered our usual dinners, two chicken tacos, rice and beans, and two of the best margaritas you will ever have. Creatures of habit, I guess.

I suddenly heard, "Hey Drew! Oh, you must be Liz. Drew has told me so much about you," as JT pulled out a chair and sat down at our table. I was shocked and unsure what to say because I hadn't told Liz about the Program or the offer yet. *What the hell is this guy doing?* raced through my mind.

Liz was puzzled and a little taken aback, then took it in her stride, smiling and shaking his hand. "Pleased to meet you, sir," she said with enthusiasm.

"Babe, I work with JT. He's a sergeant at the police department," I said, struggling for an explanation.

"Oh, okay. Do you live around here?" Liz asked. "Drew doesn't talk much about work, but he loves it and can't wait to go in every day."

"You are even more beautiful than he described you," JT said as he moved in closer to her. "Really? Well that's very nice of you," Liz said, throwing me a look.

"Hey listen, I don't want to bother you two love birds, I have to run. Drew, you wouldn't happen to have that paperwork I left with you, would you?" JT asked.

Shocked, I really didn't know how to answer his question. This son-of-a-bitch doesn't want me to tell anyone, yet he fronts me off right here in the middle of Don Jose's on my day off in front of my girlfriend? Seriously? I was pissed inside and Liz could sense it.

"Yeah, Sarge, it's in my car," I told him.

"Would you mind, Junior?" JT said with a smile. "It was so nice to meet you and sorry for interrupting your dinner. Can I see that beautiful smile one more time before I leave?" he asked Liz.

Liz looked at me as if to ask if this guy was for real. "Ahh, you are too kind and it's no problem at all. Have a good night sir." Her smile widened as her eyes sparkled.

As I walked outside with JT to give him my paperwork, JT said, "Wow, Junior, she is some nice piece of ass. Are you sure you want to leave that?" He started to laugh. "I wouldn't leave that if I was you."

34

I was pissed inside and trying to control my emotions so I didn't respond. I got to my truck and retrieved the paperwork from my backpack. When I turned to hand it to JT, he had a grin on his face that I couldn't explain. It brought instant uncontrollable anger to my body. I really just wanted to punch him in the face. "JT, is this how it's going to be? You following me, flirting with my girlfriend, and messing with me all the time? Playing these stupid little games. Is that what you do?" I asked as I finally lost my temper.

"What did you say, Junior? Did you just lose your mind? Who do you think you are talking to?" JT snapped back.

"I don't know who I'm talking to except some crazy man that likes to fuck with me. If you want me, then train me, but don't fuck with me, especially in front of my girlfriend on my day off," my mouth continued to run.

JT started laughing hysterically. "Junior, you just passed your first test. Have a good night and enjoy your dinner," he said as he walked away. "Junior, I'll see you tomorrow morning at 0800 hours at Headquarters. Wait in the lobby until someone gets you."

"JT, that's it? Wait," I yelled, but he just kept walking. Suddenly, I saw a car's lights turn on from the north and the vehicle started driving

35

towards him. The car stopped and he got in the passenger side and the vehicle pulled away. The windows were tinted, but as the vehicle turned, I saw a female driver. She had long dark brown hair but I really couldn't make out any other features. As I walked back into the restaurant to face Liz, I was trying to decide whether this was the right time to tell her. I chose not to.

Tomorrow No. 2

0600 hours – I finished my shift from the night before and I was tired. I just wanted to go home. Rivas and I had been on a child abuse case all night and mentally I was drained. The drive from my assigned station to Headquarters Division was short. When I pulled up in front of Headquarters, I was a little intimidated I must say. I grew up watching Adam 12 and worked so hard to become a policeman and now here I was parked in front of Headquarters, the heartbeat of the city. If you've never seen Headquarters, it's an enormous police facility located in the heart of downtown. It's iconic. As I was walking up to the building, I couldn't help but think of all the legendary heroic police officers that had passed through its doors. I took a deep breath as I walked into the building and tried to calm my nerves. I generally get nervous before big tests or events but not this bad. My hands were sweating profusely. I didn't know if I was about to blow the biggest opportunity or get accepted into the biggest mistake of my life.

Eight o'clock arrived and I didn't see JT around. I decided to get a cup of coffee, even though I didn't drink coffee. I attempted to choke it down, desperately seeking a jolt of caffeine to help me wake up and give me some energy for the interview. I have never been a morning person and the previous night's shift was definitely taking its toll. JT arrived a little late, walking past the armed guard located at the front lobby and greeting me with his usual small talk. I perked up, putting on my best smile and interview personality. JT escorted me past the guard to a set of elevators which went up and down every day passing several floors housing some of the greatest police divisions in the world.

Just as the elevator doors were about to close, a tall thin black man made his way onto the elevator. He appeared larger than life to me. He was tall, his uniform was pressed, shoes shined, and he commanded a presence of confidence or cockiness; which one I wasn't sure. He had a few stars on his collar but I didn't count them. As he walked in with his entourage, we locked eyes; neither of us said a word as he turned his head. JT greeted him, "Chief," and nodded.

"JT," the Chief nodded in acknowledgement, then exited at the next floor.

"Junior, that was Deputy Chief Bernard Paris. Next time you greet him as *Sir* first. He's an arrogant son-of-a-bitch and he likes his ass kissed. Don't cross him or he will fuck you," JT explained.

"Yes sir, good to know," I said.

As we arrived on our floor, we exited the elevator and walked down a narrow corridor. This corridor dead ended at a single door which you needed a security clearance and a combination to access. JT entered his combination and escorted me through the door. My stomach began to tighten a little as we walked past several desks. The office was filled with little cubbyholes, each with their own desks, but nothing too fancy. It didn't appear that a large-scale covert operation was running out of here. JT took me to a back room and told me to have a seat. The room was similar to a conference room, with a couple of tables put together with chairs. JT left the room and I began to scan my surroundings looking for anything that could help ease my curiosity. The room was pretty dull: a Raiders poster was hanging on one wall and a few nondescript pictures, but nothing out of the ordinary. Then I saw a stack of photos which appeared to be Academy classes lying on one of the tables. I assumed that was part of the background process. Just as I got up to take a closer look, the door opened and in came JT.

"Junior, some detectives are going to come in and ask you some questions. Just answer them honestly. You will be here about two hours and then I'll come back in to get you. Do you have to take a piss or do you want something to drink?" JT naturally barked.

"Okay, sounds good. I'll take something to drink if I'm going to be here two hours," I said, trying to conceal my dismay at the timeline.

"What do you want?" JT asked.

"What do you have?" I asked.

"I have scotch, water, or a combination of both," JT answered.

"Water is fine, thanks," I replied, wondering, *Is this guy for real? Scotch?*

JT left to go get my water. This time when he returned six other people followed him into the room. As they entered, they all introduced themselves to me, seven in all: JT, Jack, Albert, Jayson, Claire, Samantha, and David. I was sitting at the head of the table and JT positioned himself directly across from me. Jack sat on JT's right side

39

with Samantha on his left. Al sat on my right side, Claire to my left then Jayson and David in the middle seats. I could feel all their eyes, years of experience and rank, all focused on me; a probationary police officer with only two months of patrol under my belt. I felt a bit uneasy. I figured they were looking for an undercover officer with a cool head, so I began to focus on my heart rate and breathing. However, on the inside my heart rate was elevated and not tricked by my masking techniques as my nerves raced. The interview began with them asking some general questions about my background such as my employment history and previous residences.

As the interview continued, randomly someone would ask a question with no commonality that I could decipher, but I would classify them as more informational than challenging or technical.

Albert was sitting directly to my right; his legs were crossed and he had glasses hanging off the tip of his nose. He was an older gentleman with slicked-back hair, brown and grey in color, thinning, with a partial comb-over in play. He reminded me of Jack Nicholson with a constant or a resting *dick* look on his face. He was wearing a lime-green collared shirt that was stretched by a larger-than-healthy belly, tucked into brown slacks. His shoes were black, but scuffed at the toes, and in desperate need of polish. The sole of his right shoe was worn more than his left, as if he dragged his foot slightly when he walked. His socks were lime green and he smelled like Old Spice cologne, one of my father's favorites. He hadn't asked me any questions yet, but his eyes were locked on my every word and move, making me nervous. His stare was as if he was looking through me. It was uncomfortable and gave off a definite confrontational vibe.

Albert sat up in his chair and unfolded his arms. "Drew, in this assignment you are required to give up your badge, gun, and police identity for the extent of your assignment. You said that becoming a police officer was a very important part of your life. Can you give that up?" He leaned forward and his eyes crossed in an intimidating way, awaiting my response.

I paused, because I had never really thought about this assignment in that manner.

"Drew, did you hear my question?" Albert asked after a while.

"I did, sir. I won't give up being a police officer. It's something I worked too hard to give up."

JT uncrossed his legs and leaned towards me. "Are you changing your mind about being in the program?" His scowl appeared.

41

I paused again before answering, "No, sir, I'm not changing my mind, but I don't see me going undercover as giving up being a police officer. I will always be a police officer in my heart, so I don't necessarily have to identify myself with the equipment or symbols associated with a police officer."

"Drew, what does your family think about your decision?" asked David.

"I'm not sure, sir, but I know they would be concerned but supportive," I responded.

"You haven't told your family yet?" David asked me with a puzzled look.

"No, I won't tell them until I know that I have been accepted into the program. No sense for them to worry or ask me a thousand questions that I don't know the answers to until it's a done deal," I responded.

Claire, who was sitting to my left, seemed like a gentle spirit and definitely did not look like an officer. She looked more like my grandma or kindergarten teacher. The questions she would ask were simple and her body language would almost applaud my answers.

Samantha was the youngest of the crew by far, and the lowest rank too, I assumed by her demeanor. I believe I recognized her as the girl who had been driving the car that night when JT had surprised me at Don Jose's when I was with Liz. Her hair was dark, shoulder-length with a slight wave. She was wearing a business suit that hugged her body. Her breasts were full, perky and large. Her eyes squinted when she smiled. I guessed she was half Hispanic and half Asian.

"Drew, I see your mom worked for the CIA years ago. What did she do?" asked Jayson.

"I'm not really sure, but it wasn't anything major and she never really talked much about it. I know she was stationed in Germany for a time," I answered.

Jayson seemed concerned about my mom's employment with the *Agency*, twenty-five years prior. "Drew, do you think your mom would use her CIA contacts to try and find you while you are undercover?" he continued to inquire.

A broken smile came across my face quickly, and Jayson caught it. "Drew, what's the smirk about?" Jayson looked like a gray-haired Jesus to me. His hair was long, straggly and white. He was dressed casually, but his hands were rough and calloused as if he had worked hard throughout his life. He had long gray chest hair playing peek-a-boo from under his Hawaiian shirt.

"No, sir, my mom doesn't have any CIA contacts anymore. Her employment with the *Agency* wasn't that long and it wasn't like that. Besides, you don't know my mom. If she wanted to find me, she wouldn't need the CIA's help," I explained. The intensity in the room broke just a little, as there were a few chuckles.

Albert leaned forward. "Drew, let's say you are accepted into the program and you are working as an undercover with your group. Your group decides to go do a 211 at a bank. What do you do?"

I paused. A 211 was a robbery. "I would call my supervisor and advise them of the situation."

"Let me be clearer, Drew, your group already picked you up and you are on your way to do the 211 and you don't have a phone. They tell you, this is your final test. If you don't do this 211 with us, we will kill you." Albert stared at me intensely as he finished his question.

My inside voice started to talk: *Albert, you're a son-of-a -bitch, what would you do, asshole? I don't really know what I would do. Aren't you guys supposed to train me in this undercover crap.*

"Albert, can you repeat the question please?" I asked, hoping my stalling would give me just a little more time for an answer to pop into my head. "I would try and stall my group or have them put off the 211 to another time so that I could notify my supervisors of their intentions," I finally said. *Whew, that was a good answer, that ought to satisfy this old fart.*

"What would you say to stall them?" Albert quickly shot back.

Calmly I said, "I would tell them we need to plan it out so we don't get caught." I finished my sentence with a silent *"asshole"* in my head.

This cat and mouse game went back and forth for several series of scenarios regarding the 211. Then Albert said, "Okay, none of your stall tactics worked, you had to go inside with your group, as they enter the bank and they shoot the guard. What do you do? Do you identify yourself as a police officer?"

During our banter about this question, I had anticipated the scenario was going to go this way so I had already thought about my answers.

"How many of my group are inside with me and how many are in the car?" I asked.

"Two are inside with you and there is one driver," Albert quickly responded.

"Am I armed?" I asked.

"Sure, with a 9mm." Albert's smirk widened.

"I shoot the two members of my group inside the bank, then identify myself as an undercover officer. I have someone call 911 while I observe the driver."

A deafening silence came across the room as the tension grew. My eyes were locked on Albert, but I could feel everyone looking at me. Out of the corner of my eye, David cracked a slight smile, JT leaned back in his chair and crossed his legs.
Albert turned his head and looked at JT. His head nodded, in a downward motion that caused his glasses to almost fall off his nose. He stood up and shook my hand and thanked me for coming in. The rest of the group followed his lead and exited the room.

"Junior, just sit tight. I'll be back for you." JT put his hand on my shoulder and left the room. He returned about fifteen minutes later and escorted me back to my car. I didn't ask him the obvious question and he didn't offer any enlightenment.

"Junior, I'll get hold of you in a couple of days," he said.

"I'm sure you will," I replied with a sarcastic undertone, knowing he wasn't going to give me any information.

About three days went by and I finally received a phone call from JT. He advised me that he wanted me to come in and have an interview with the Lieutenant and the Captain of the Division. He'd set up the interview for the following day at 0800 hours and told me that my background was completed and everything was fine.

So the next day, I drove back to Headquarters at the end of my shift and waited in the lobby for JT again. He arrived on time this time, but there was a slightly different feel about him this morning. He actually seemed a little nervous as he began to brief me on my upcoming interview with the command staff. It was almost as if he was coaching me.

"Junior, first you'll meet with the Lieutenant. He'll ask you some minor questions, but nothing difficult. He really just wants to know if you know what you are signing up to do and that you want to do it. After that you'll meet with the Captain and he'll ask you very similar questions. Don't be nervous and keep your answers short. Don't talk too much," JT rambled, a side of him I had never seen before.

As we walked into the elevators, I was a little disappointed that I didn't see any Deputy Chiefs. We walked down the narrow corridor and

I wasn't as nervous as the previous time. JT punched in his security code and we walked past the same cubbyholes again.

"Hi Drew, welcome back," said Sam with a big smile as I walked towards the conference room, only answering her with a nod of my head.

"Junior, take a seat. The Lieutenant will be in and remember what I told you," JT said. His nerves were obvious but I really couldn't understand why.

"Yes sir, I got it," I tried to assure him.

A few minutes went by and the door flew open. "Junior, let's go. The Captain wants to see you now," JT barked.

Now I began to get nervous. As a young police officer this was my first encounter with a police captain. JT escorted me to the captain's office and introduced me to Captain John Adams. The Captain had a vertically-challenged but athletic build and was fairly young looking. He welcomed me as we all sat at a small round table located in his office. He then gave me an overview of the program which took him about ten minutes before he began to talk about his kids. He went on talking about his kids for about fifteen more minutes, concluding with, "Drew, are you sure you want to enter into the program?"

"I am sure, sir," I said, making certain I looked him in the eyes just as JT had coached me.

"Great! Thanks for coming in and good luck to you," the Captain said as he stood up to shake my hand. Then JT escorted me out of the office and back down to the lobby. The interview was short and sweet. Once again, I didn't ask the obvious question and JT didn't offer any information. As I was leaving the lobby, I said, "I know: you'll get hold of me," beating JT to the punch.

"You got that right, Junior." JT shook his head and turned back inside.

JT called me the next day and told me I had to come up to Headquarters again for a second interview. I went through the same procedures – lobby, elevator, corridor, JT's speech, ending up in the conference room – the whole process definitely getting old to me.

I heard JT through the door: "Lieutenant, do you have time to interview MacGregor today? Captain spoke with him yesterday, but I wanted you to speak with him."

A loud voice replied, "If the Captain has already spoken to him, JT, I don't need to talk to him. I'm not going to disagree with the Captain." He appeared to walk away.

The conference room door opened, and JT said, "Junior, I guess you didn't have to come down today, I'm sorry." He actually seemed apologetic for my obvious inconvenience. As we were walking back down to the lobby, this time I asked the obvious. "So, what are my chances and when will I know if I got the job?"

"Junior, you'll know by Monday. It's down to you and another candidate, but I'm pulling for you."

"Sounds good, thanks JT," I said, and left Headquarters this time thinking I'd got the job.

Monday

At 1022 hours my phone rang, waking me up.

"Hello?" I said, still half asleep having worked all night.

"Welcome to the program, Junior. You got the job," JT exclaimed. I acted like I'd known all along I was going to get it, but inside I was saying, *Holy shit, I got it.*

"Starting January 22, your ass is mine," JT said. "We'll talk soon."

Now I was a little scared, because at this point, I didn't know anything about this job. The only thing that I knew was that I had just lost three years of my life and now I had to tell my family and Liz.

July 1994

My sister was down from Northern California to visit me for my birthday. I was renting a house just outside of Los Angeles with my best friend Gary and had just finished my twelfth week in the police academy.

"Hey Sis, we have to go to the grocery store for dinner tonight, do you want to go with me?" I asked.

"Sure." She flipped her curly hair to the right to get it out of her face and grabbed her sunglasses.

We drove to the local Vons Grocery Store where we picked up a few things for dinner. "Oh, there she is. Hey, sis, there is my future wife right there." I jokingly motioned my head towards the third check-out lane.

"Your future wife? Which one?" she asked.

"The hot little Hispanic girl right there. I think her name is Liz. Liz MacGregor? How do you think that sounds?"

"Wow, she's cute. So that's why we passed two other grocery stores and came here?" As my sister shook her head at me, I started to laugh.

"If that's going to be your wife, did you tell her yet?" my sis asked.

"Tell her what, that she's going to be my wife?" I asked, puzzled.

"Yes, did you tell her that yet?"

"No, you're crazy. I wouldn't tell her that, besides she has a ring on," I responded.

"That ring could be fake. Just ask her out, you big scaredy cat!" my sister held her ground.

"Girls wear fake wedding rings? Really, why would they do that?" I mumbled to myself, still perplexed by my sis's statement. We waited in Liz's line like I always did. She knew who I was, but she didn't know my name.

"Hey Liz," I greeted her as usual.

"Oh, hi, how are you? I haven't seen you in a while," she said, laughing nervously.

"This is my sister; she's visiting me from up north," I introduced them.

"Oh hi! My name is Liz. It's very nice to meet you," she said as she extended her greeting hand.

"Well, you're right, brother; she is cute as a button," my sis said as she looked at me. Devastated, I couldn't believe my sis had just let her inner voice out.

Liz responded with a big smile, "Ahh, you are too sweet. Thank you! Drew – it *is* Drew, right? – did you really say that?" Liz asked with confidence.

I stumbled trying to find words, not knowing how to respond since my sister had put me on *blast*.

"Well… I did… Wait, you know my name?" I asked.

"He brought me here because he wanted me to meet you, his future wife, he says," my sister continued to run her mouth as my embarrassment hit an all-time high.
"That's what he said."

Liz turned and looked at me again. Her smile widened as it lit up the room.

"Well, Drew, if we're going to get married, I think you should call me first, don't you?" Liz said, with intimidating confidence. She pulled out a black marker from her smock and wrote her phone number on the back of the grocery receipt. "Here's my number, I get off at six," She said as her face brightened.

"That's a deal. I'll call you," I promised her.

As sis and I walked out of the store, my heart was racing and I couldn't believe what had just happened. It seemed so simple, so why had I let my fear of rejection paralyze me for the past two months? As we walked out of the store, I took one last look back at Liz... "You're welcome brother," my sister said as she shook her head.

That night, Liz and I began a whirlwind romance. She was a traditional Hispanic woman who believed in traditional gender roles. Her main ambition in life was to get married, serve her husband, and have lots of children; not necessarily in that order. Standing five-foot-four and weighing all of a-hundred-and-three pounds, she had dark hair, and her body was blessed with the smoothest complexion I'd ever seen. One *angel kiss* on her left butt cheek, and a two-inch scar from a dog bite when she was eight on her right leg were her only blemishes. Bangs to cover what she believed to be a larger-than-normal forehead, snow-white teeth with a perfect smile, eyes that sparkled with excitement; always looking for a chance to dress up to show off her backside, which as it turned out was her favorite feature, as it was mine. She had a soft heart, sensitive, but was never afraid to laugh or take herself too seriously. Looking for any and every opportunity to please me, just because she wanted to, not looking for anything in return. Shy at moments, yet fearless in a crowd. However, her most admirable quality was that she was full of life and didn't care what other people thought.

Talking for hours about nothing on some nights, walking in the rain with our clothes drenched, not even caring, watching what I thought were our favorite movies over and over, snuggled on the couch, only later to find out she hated them.

Liz was the first woman in my life who had put me first in the relationship. It was strange, awesome, and yet uncomfortable to me at times; it was a role reversal for me. Liz truly just wanted to take care of my needs first because that's what made her happy.

On the day I graduated from the police academy, Liz took the day off to attend. I was standing at attention, feet together, with my fists clasped at my sides, waiting for the Chief to pin my badge on my chest. I scanned the crowd without trying to move my head. There she was, in a tight purple dress I had never seen before that hugged her body, stopping mid-thigh. As she struggled to walk across the academy grass grounds in three-inch-high heels, heads turned as she made her way towards an open area on the track looking for a place to view the ceremony. After the ceremony, she found me in the crowd and I took her to meet my parents.

"It's so nice to meet my future in-laws," Liz said with a big smile.

My mom was somewhat taken back. "You must be Liz. It's nice to meet you too, hun." Everyone was there: my parents, sister and my closest friends. It was a great moment in my life.

Later that night, Liz and I went out to dinner with my sister and my mom and on the way home as I was driving her back to my house, Liz said, "I'm so proud of you, babe. Now we can start our lives together and get married."

"Married? Really? You want to get married right now?" I responded.

"Sure, why not? We love each other and you said you were going to marry me when you first saw me, right? That's what you said, Drew."

I didn't answer back as I was trying to process what exactly was happening.

"Why? Now you don't want to get married?" Liz looked patiently in my eyes.

"That's not what I said, Liz. We've only been dating five months. Marriage is for life, there isn't a rush."

Her head turned to me. "You must not love me the way I love you, because I already know that you are the only one I want to marry. It's okay, I know you will come around. I will show you. Are you up for ice cream?" she said, quickly switching topic.

"Sure, only if there's mint-n-chip," I responded quickly, relieved.

A couple of weeks later, I finished my shift on patrol and got home around 0730 in the morning like I usually did, and went to sleep. I woke up and immediately recognized the smell of *albondigas* soup. I stumbled out of bed and saw Liz in my kitchen.

"I'm sorry, did I wake you?" she asked.

"No, but is that smell what I think it is?" I said, beginning to get excited.

"It is, but you need to get your butt back to bed, it's not quite ready and you are going to ruin my plan," Liz insisted.

"No, it's okay, babe..."

Liz cut me off. "Seriously, get your butt back to bed!" Her smile turned to a stern look and her Latina side came out as she began to rattle off a bunch of Spanish words I didn't understand. I had no idea what she said, but I knew what to do, immediately turning around and crawling back into bed where I quickly dozed back off to sleep. I woke up this time to a cold body crawling on top of me with soft wet kisses on my neck.

"I missed you last night and I couldn't wait to see you. I called Gary and he left me a key. I hope you don't mind," she whispered softly.

"No. Are you kidding me? I wake up to a hot, naked Mexican girl in my bed and you think I'm going to be mad?"

"Hey, what about the soup?" Liz giggled.

"Oh, yeah. I forgot about the soup." We began to laugh.

"You need to serve me first then I will serve you your soup." Her head disappeared under the sheets.

Later, we climbed out of bed and were enjoying my favorite soup. "Hey, let's go to Vegas. We've never been to Vegas together," she said as her face lit up.

"Right now? We don't have any reservations," I responded while looking at her like she was crazy.

"Mac, you don't need a plan for everything in life. It will be okay; don't worry, I will protect you." She batted her eyelids at me and laughed. "Come on. Please… Do you want to pack a bag or do you want me to pack one for you?" she continued.

"Okay, let's do it," I said, out of character. "You can pack one for me if you want. Let me see if I can get a room," I yelled out.

"No, we'll figure it out when we get there. No plans, Mac. I'm going to go home and pack. Can you pick me up in a half hour?" she yelled as she ran out the door before I could change my mind.

Before I knew it, Liz and I were Vegas bound. Looking back on it, we were in our early twenties with no real responsibilities or obligations at the time. We just left and didn't tell a soul. There wasn't any arranging of baby sitters; missing a kid's sporting event; or parents to ask or tell, for that matter. No time schedule, no plans, and no real financial obligations. Just time and money to burn.

"Let's go to Caesar's," she suggested.

"Okay, I love Caesar's too." We valet parked and gave our bags to the bell hop.

"Follow me; this is my tradition. We have to place a hundred dollars on black before we do anything," she said with excitement.

"Really? Why, a hundred dollars and why on black?" I asked.

"I always do. It's a sign of how much fun I'm going to have," Liz responded.

"You're crazy, but now you are in my world, babe. The MacGregors are gamblers. You choose which roulette table and I'll take it from there."

"Not that one, female Asian dealers are not lucky. That one! He looks nice," Liz said.

"Okay, you said black, right? Why black?" I asked.

"Don't you know, once you go black you never go back?" she said as she started laughing.

"Okay, black it is. Five hundred on black." I upped the ante.

"Mac, you are crazy. Don't do that. That is too much." Liz's conservative side was coming out.

"What's your lucky number?" I asked her, shocked I didn't already know the answer.

"Nineteen, my birthday of course," she said as if I should've known that by now.

"Can I have a hundred on nineteen and a hundred on seven?" I asked as I threw down two more hundred-dollar-bills.

"Money plays, no more bets!" the attendant screamed. The wheel spinning, Liz grabbed my hand and my heart beat quickly, but I didn't let on. My hands began to sweat but that was the only indicator that I was nervous.

"Come on, black! Black! Black! Black!" Liz yelled and jumped up and down. It was worth every penny just to see the excitement in her eyes and to witness a beautiful woman living life to the fullest.

Clack, clack, clack. My eyes tried to track the ball bouncing on the wheel as it slowed to reveal the outcome. The ball bounced upward one last time in between two red numbers. It bounced and hit the divider and fell on the next number over to the right.

"Nineteen, black!" the attendant yelled and Liz jumped into my arms as we embraced in a passionate kiss. The attendant called the pit boss over as he counted out our winnings.

"Thirty-five-hundred, sir! Nice hit!" Liz and I were still in shock as he gave me colors of chips I had never seen before.

The pit boss came over to us. "Are you staying with us, sir?"

"We just got here and we would love to stay with you. Do you have any suites?" I asked him.

"I'm sure we do but I can't comp you a suite." He knew I had just got lucky and I wasn't a whale of a gambler.

"We want a suite for two nights, what can you do?" I asked him.

"I can put you in the executive suite for five-hundred a night," he responded.

"Let's do it. Thank you," I said as I gave Liz a big hug.

"Yes sir, and I'll throw in some show tickets for you too," he said as he walked away.

"I can't believe it! You did it!" Liz was still gleaming with excitement.

"No, we did it. Liz, let's have some fun," I said.

Liz and I checked into the suite and had the time of our lives. Over the next two days and nights we had great dinners, wine, conversation, shopping sprees, pool-side lounging, and pushed the lines of excitement all without gambling another dime. The second night we were sitting on the balcony of our suite overlooking the strip.

"I will be back," Liz yelled and I didn't think much about it. I was content smoking my cigar, drinking scotch, and soaking up the wonderful views. I couldn't be happier.

Several minutes later, I heard a knock at our door but I didn't get up.

Knock, knock, knock. I heard the door again so I got up. "Liz? Is that the door?" I called out. She didn't answer me. I looked around, but I didn't see her. *Knock, knock.* "Room service."

Not knowing we'd ordered room service, I answered the door. Liz was standing in the hallway, her hair pulled back, black push-up bra displaying the majority of the most perfect but small breasts you could imagine, smooth tan skin with a belly button piercing, black thigh-high stockings with a garter belt, and black three-inch high heels, holding a tray of chocolate-covered strawberries and a bottle of champagne.

"Room service, sir," she said while still standing in the hallway for anyone to see. Shocked, excited, and stunned, I quickly pulled her inside our suite so no one else could see what I had.

"What are you doing? Someone could see you! I can't believe you. Are you crazy?" I said quickly, my heart still racing. She didn't say anything and continued to walk out to the balcony where we had been sitting. The high heels made her calves pop as she walked towards the balcony. Her exposed backside moved side to side as she looked back at me. I followed her and began to salivate like Pavlov's dog. She set the tray of chocolate strawberries down on a small table on the balcony next to the chair where I was sitting.

"Have a seat, Mac, and don't say a word. Here are the rules. You can't talk or touch me unless I tell you to," she said in a very seductive, yet serious voice. "Do you understand the rules?"

"What?" I said nervously.

She slapped me lightly across the face. "I said no talking," she said with a serious look on her face.

She walked back into the suite and turned on some music. Then she walked back out to the balcony and started to dance there I was looking around to see if anyone was watching what I was watching. I couldn't believe what was happening. Things like this didn't happen to me and I didn't think Liz was one to go for things like this either. It was another side of her that I hadn't seen before and I was loving it. Liz seductively danced around for the next fifteen minutes, losing a piece of clothing one at a time until she was completely naked. She pulled a chair closer to me and began to pleasure herself to orgasm in front of me right there on the balcony.

"Liz, there are people right there!" I said.

"I told you no talking! I'm sure they won't mind because I don't."

"I would be stupid not to marry you," I said in a moment of weakness.

"I told you that you would come around." Liz smiled.

Flap Your Wings

"With foxes we must play the fox."

Thomas Fuller

JT told me that on January 22 my name would appear on the department transfer sheet reassigning me from patrol to *Personnel Division* and that I was never to tell anyone that I had been assigned to this division. JT said to slowly start to empty my locker out so that no one would be suspicious about me leaving. He could sense my nerves a little bit and told me he would never identify any previous birds, but he would in this one case.

"Junior, there is a lieutenant by the name of Kelly that works day watch; he worked the program several years ago. You can talk to him and tell him that I sent you. He can answer any questions you might have."

"Lieutenant Kelly on Days shift? Okay, I'll talk to him, thanks," I answered.

The following day at the end of the watch, I looked for Lt. Kelly who happened to be sitting at the Watch Commander's desk as I walked in to turn in my log from the previous night's patrol.

"Excuse me sir, my name is MacGregor. Could I talk to you about something when you have a minute?" I asked.

"Go ahead, MacGregor, what do you need?" Lt. Kelly said, appearing somewhat bothered by my request.

"Sir, I need to speak with you in private. JT sent me," I responded as my voice cracked.

"JT sent you?" Lt. Kelly said, raising his head. "Sure, MacGregor, let's go up to the Captain's office." We walked up to the Captain's office and he shut the door. "So how is that old crusty motherfucker JT? He's still up to his secret squirrel shit I see." Lt. Kelly put his feet up on the Captain's desk as he leaned back in his chair. He reached into the right drawer of the Captain's desk and pulled out a bottle of scotch and two glasses.

"Scotch, MacGregor?" he asked as he poured himself a finger.

"No thank you, sir."

"Good answer. Wait until you get off probation and then they can't touch you," he said as he took a sip of scotch.

The lieutenant was a very unusual man. A towering black man with hands that swallowed mine as we shook. He spoke calmly with a monotone voice. His skin was dark and he had a small eye-twitch that kept distracting me when he spoke. He spoke for several minutes about the program but didn't really tell me anything. It brought back memories of me in med school studying for a test; I would complete the chapter but I had no idea what I just read. He had a strange look in his good eye, almost piercing. It was as if he knew what you were thinking before you did. He told me that when he was a bird he used to carry a screwdriver in his sock for protection.

"The program isn't for everyone, kid, and only a chosen few have completed it and done it well. If you go into the program it will change you as a person and you will forever be looking over your shoulder. Do you believe that, kid? That it will forever change your life?" The lieutenant dropped his feet from the desk and leaned forward with a death-stare into my eyes.

"Sir, I believe what you are saying, however it is a lot to take in. Did it change your life for the better?" I asked.

"Sure, but as with everything in life, there's some good and some bad," the lieutenant answered honestly.

"Sir, would you do it again?" I asked.

"You know, I'm not sure. That was a long time ago and I tend not to second- guess my decisions once I make them and I suggest you do the same." The lieutenant took another sip of scotch.

"Okay, thanks for the advice," I answered as I stood up.

"Hey kid, there's no shame in changing your mind on this. It's probably one of the most important decisions you will be faced with in life. Do you have any more questions?"

"Can I die… I mean, have any birds been killed in the program?" I asked, which I had never really considered prior to this moment.

"That's a question for JT, kid," the lieutenant answered as he finished his scotch, then stood up and offered his hand.

The next day I reported to work as usual and went through my routine getting dressed. Superstitiously, I would always get dressed a certain way, but it worked for me. I would always finish by checking my 9mm to make sure it was loaded; put my back-up weapon, a .38 caliber, in my pocket; and my knife in my left boot preparing for battle. After roll call, I gathered the equipment and prepped the car for patrol before Rivas came outside. Rivas had over twenty years on the job, all of which had been spent working the streets. He was old-school LAPD. He wasn't very big, standing at five-foot-nine, but he was in excellent shape, often choosing to pump some iron instead of eating on his lunch break. He was the toughest training officer in the division, but the word was amongst the rookies, if he gave you the nod the remaining part of your probation was smooth sailing.

It was a Tuesday. Rivas was very quiet but I didn't dare ask him if everything was okay. Rivas was driving as usual because he never trusted any boots to drive during the first phase of training. He drove up to the north end of the division, which was strange because it was out of our assigned area. It was cold that night and a fog was hugging the hills. He turned into a small park that I hadn't even known existed and parked the car.

"Get out and don't put us Code 6," he said as he exited the car.

He sounded pissed so I quickly exited the car. As I got out he was already in my face.

"What the hell did you talk to Kelly about in the Captain's office for an hour? Are you trying to beef me, Junior? You are fucking with the wrong guy," he spat, his steel-black eyes locked on mine. I actually almost peed myself out of fear.

Caught off guard and scared, I wasn't sure what to say. I knew if I tried to bullshit him, he'd see through it, however I also knew that JT had said if I told anyone I would be kicked out of the program. I quickly understood the magnitude of the situation that I was in… Rivas thought that I was breaking the code of silence often referred to in the public eye and mainstream media as a boot. I chose to tell Rivas the truth mainly out of fear because I honestly felt he was going to kill me.

"Sir, I wouldn't beef you. It's just a personal problem that I'm going through and I needed to take some time off," I said.

"Bullshit. You're going to tell me right now or I'm going to kick your ass," Rivas exclaimed and I believed him.

"Sir, it's not about you I swear. It's just a personal problem and I needed his help." My second feeble attempt at an explanation.

"Do you think I'm stupid, Junior? He's not even your lieutenant and you didn't go to your den sergeant like you were supposed to. You went straight to Kelly who used to work Internal Affairs. Are you a snitch, Junior?" Scared, realizing I was out of time, I spilled the beans.

"Sir, I was offered an undercover job at a special division and I was sent to Kelly to ask him about the program, because he worked it back in the day. That's it, I swear," I said in desperation.

"No shit!" He took a step back and I could see the pulse in his neck vein begin to calm. "Junior, you have a lot to learn about being undercover," he said as he started to laugh. "My first tip to you is next time you want to talk to Kelly don't just walk into the Watch Commander's office and say, 'Hey, Lieutenant, can I talk to you in private?' and then disappear to the Captain's office for an hour. That doesn't sit too well with the troops," Rivas explained in a jovial and relieved way.

"Yes, sir. I'll remember that," I said in my own way of relief, believing that I was no longer going to die tonight, at least not at the hands of Rivas.

I was glad that I told Rivas because he had more than twenty-two years of experience and he gave me his opinion on what I should do. Rivas said that I would be stupid not to take the job and that it was a once in a life time opportunity for me. He said generally you have to know someone to work in or get an offer from that division and that it was considered one of the most elite units in the Department. I was relieved to hear that from Rivas, because he was a straight-up kind of guy and I knew that if he thought the job was crap, he would spill it.

Over the next few days, I spoke to JT every day and he would advise me of certain general administrative duties regarding my transition. As the days neared for my transfer, I was definitely sad and I had a lot of mixed emotions about leaving patrol. I was just starting to get the hang of it and it was a ton of fun. I had developed a good rapport with the officers and one particular assistant Watch Commander,

Sergeant Shoop. He was an old-timer but he actually treated boots with some respect instead of as the usual pond scum. He gave me the moniker *Professor*. I'd earned the nickname because when a *boot* turns in a report for review or approval by a supervisor, it is highly scrutinized for any errors. I prided myself on an accurate report and Shoop could never find any errors on mine.

"Professor, come here. You finally have a kickback," he said as he handed me the report with a smile and showed me that I had a misspelled word. I looked at the report to see what word I had misspelled but I knew that the word was spelled right. I double-checked the spelling in the old Webster's Dictionary before I turned it back in to Shoop.

"Sir, here's my report and I know that word is spelled correctly," I said with a smile.

"MacGregor, are you a betting man?" Shoop asked me with a smile.

"Sir, I am, but only when the odds are in my favor, sir," I replied.

"Lunch," he asked.

"Yes sir," I quickly answered.

"Get the dictionary," he commanded.

As I handed him the dictionary, I said, "Sir, it's on page 122."

Shoop just grinned and said, "You should have been a professor, MacGregor," realizing at that moment that I had already verified the spelling of the word prior to making the wager. "What do you want to eat?" he added, shaking his head as he signed the report.

January 15, 1995

"MacGregor, see the Watch Commander," echoed throughout the station over the intercom.

"Damn it! What now?" I thought, because it was never good news when a boot's name was blasted throughout the station to go see the Watch Commander. As I walked towards the office, I saw Sergeant Shoop sitting at the helm.

"Hey Sarge, did you call me?"

He leaned forward and said, "MacGregor, you are going *under the sheets*?"

"Sir?"

"You know, *under the sheets*, undercover! Your name is on the transfer list to personnel division. That has to mean only one thing, *under the sheets*. Where are you going into the schools, Juvi dope?"

75

Shoop inquired, referring to an undercover program that was widely known thanks to the television show, *21 Jump Street*, and a reasonable deduction, considering my baby face.

"Not sure, sir," I responded.

"No one has talked to you?" he asked.

"No sir," I said, feeling bad inside about lying to him.

The next day at roll call Shoop said, "MacGregor I need to see you after roll call." At this point officers began to wonder why I was getting so much attention and began to distance themselves from me. They were beginning to think that I was some kind of a problem child or an internal affairs plant, which was always an ongoing fear amongst the troops. I walked into the Watch Commander's office and Shoop said, "MacGregor you could have told me."

"Sir?" I asked, hoping that pleading ignorance could save me.

"MacGregor, I know. Yesterday after you told me you didn't know about the transfer, I started to make a few phone calls to help you out. Next thing I know, I get a call from the Chief's office telling me to let it go. That doesn't happen unless you are going one place, that I didn't even know still existed," Shoop explained.

"Sir, my apologies. You have been nothing but good to me, but I was told not to say anything to anyone."

"I know you can't talk about it, but look me up when you get out. I'll buy you a beer and I would love to hear about it someday. Watch your ass, MacGregor."

"I will, sir. My apologies again," I said as Shoop reached his hand out and with a firm grip shook my hand.

"Be careful out there, you hear me!"

I looked at him as a chill went up my spine. "Yes sir," I replied.

Last Night on Patrol

As Rivas and I left Tams after devouring our greasy cheeseburgers, Rivas said, "Junior. It's your night. What do you want to do?"

"I want to find Floco over on Breed Street."

Floco was a Breed Street gang member who terrorized the neighborhood and I could never catch the kid dirty. Floco's MO was he liked to rob women on their way to work or to the grocery store and he was wanted for questioning on a murder. Breed Street gangsters were notorious for drive-by shootings, purse snatches, and other things like that and every time you went to jam them, it was off to the races through their obstacle course of booby traps, clotheslines, and other traps meant to hurt officers.

"You got it, call in another unit and have them meet us and let's brief them up at Tams," Rivas says.

"Roger, sir." I called for an additional unit. Approximately two minutes later, I heard the sound of engines revving and tires screeching as one unit came into our view from the south and then two more units from the east, approaching our location at high speed.

"Sir, did I call that in wrong?" I asked, thinking I must have messed something up.

"No, Junior, you did it right. It's just I never ask for an additional unit so when I do, everyone treats it like an officer needs help call." He started to chuckle, but what came out didn't really qualify as a laugh.

"Scotty, I need a chase car, bud. Drive southbound on Breed for me to get these pooh-butts to run eastbound through the houses. Junior and I will be waiting there. I'll give you two chirps when we're set up. Hold your position there for me until I call you," Rivas told him.

"You got it, Rivas! Want me to have one of the other units for the north?" Scotty asked.

"Negative! We got it," Rivas said as he turned to get in the car. "Junior, you're driving. Pull to the north end of Breed, black out, and park. Silence your gear and follow me."

I couldn't believe I was driving as I parked the car and we walked southbound. A dog started to bark, but we kept walking. Rivas jumped a block wall and I followed him. He motioned me to set up on one side of the house while he set up on the other side. He gave me the thumbs up and I heard two chirps from the radio in my earpiece. I saw the black and white come to a screeching halt to my west.

"Po Po! Po Po!" an unknown voice yelled out. I saw several pooh-butts running in our direction. Two were running right at me, but they hadn't seen me yet. "Stop, police," I yelled. The two pooh-butts split up and I tackled one guy as the other got away. I looked up and another pooh-butt turned towards Rivas who had his side-handle baton resting alongside his leg.

Crack! Rivas struck him as he ran by.

The pooh-butt screamed out in pain, "You broke my leg, motherfucker! You broke my fucking leg!"

"Turn the fuck over and put your hands behind your back, before I break your other leg," Rivas said in a calm voice.

"Fuck you," the pooh-butt yelled at Rivas.

Crack! Rivas struck his other leg. Then he flipped him over and handcuffed him. "You obviously don't know who I am, asshole. Rivas is the name."

"Rivas! Yo Rivas, I didn't know man... Ahh fuck, my leg man... I'm sorry sir, I'm sorry sir. Fuck," the pooh-butt continued.

"This little motherfucker is strapped. Junior, look what I got here." Rivas held up the gun he'd removed from the pooh-butt's waistband.

"Why are you crying like a little bitch? Are you only tough when you're picking on a woman or you need a strap?" Rivas asked. "Get up asshole, your legs aren't broken." Rivas yanked the pooh-butt up by his neck.

"My leg, fuck, fuck, fuck."

"Remember that, asshole, next time you want to run from the police. Now you know the price if you get caught, and remember, Rivas is the name." Rivas gave me the metro nod as we loaded him into the car.

It was a long night by the time we'd finished all of the paperwork. I turned in my log and went down to the locker room to change. I finished cleaning out the last few items in my locker and went to say goodbye to Rivas who was in the gym because he hadn't got his workout in at lunch.

"Sir, I'm outta here. Thanks for everything."

Rivas in classic form said, "You better hope I don't run into you out there on the streets because I will jack you up," as a grin came across his face lifting his head in the middle of bench pressing two-hundred-and-twenty-five pounds.

"I'll remember that, sir. Be safe," I said. Then as I turned to walk out, I heard him say, "Good work tonight, *partner.*" I just kept walking, but I knew I had earned some respect in Rivas's eyes.

Learning to Fly

"I am a lie who always speaks the truth."

Jean Cocteau

Training Module No. 1

"MacGregor," JT explained, "you need to call in at 0900 hours every morning and we will tell you what that day's assignment is. The first objective is to have you forget all of the stuff you just learned on the streets and in the academy. Don't use any cop lingo, or codes, don't call your classmates, don't hang out at any cop joints. You know what I mean. We also have to start to change that pretty-boy look you have going on. Don't shave and don't cut your hair. Don't wear any cop clothes, jackets, or carry any equipment associated with being a cop."

"I never had a beard or long hair before. I'm not sure I can do that," I said out loud.

"You have to, Junior; your life may depend on it. Just go through your stuff this week and get rid of or store all your cop stuff. Also, tie up any loose ends at your house if you know what I mean!" JT said.

"Sir, what do you mean?" I asked, not really knowing what he was referring to.

"You need to tell your girl what you signed up for and get rid of her. She has to go. I'm sorry, but I would recommend it sooner rather than later. Make it happen," JT reaffirmed.

For the rest of the week, I worked on deprogramming myself as a cop and went through my items as JT had advised. Every day, I would call in at 0900 hours as directed and JT would get pissed if I was a minute early or late.

0858 – "JT, it's Drew calling in."

"Junior, what time is it exactly?" JT would yell back.

"Uh, exactly? My watch says 0858," I said.

"Call me back at 0900 like I told you" – *click*, the phone was hung up. Wondering why this guy constantly liked to fuck with me, I waited until my watch said 0900 exactly, and called him back. "JT, it's exactly 0900 hours."

"Junior, you need to do exactly what I tell you to do, it may keep you alive someday. Attention to detail, son. Don't use your name anymore. We need to deprogram you."

"Okay, but how is calling in at 0900 going to save my life some day? That doesn't make any sense."

"Don't argue with me, Junior, just trust what I am saying to you and do it," JT reiterated.

Still a little frustrated with the progress of the conversation, I switched the subject. "Okay, so what's my new name?"

84

"That is on a need and right to know basis and you don't have either yet. Let's see if you make it through training first, but in the meantime, you will be given a source number which will be your name for now. Never say your real name anymore, just give your source number."

"What, like 007," I said as I started to chuckle.

"No, dumb ass, it's 36," JT fires back.

"36? Really? You're serious? Well, can I get a different number? That number doesn't sound lucky to me and I don't like it," I requested like a spoiled child.

"This isn't Burger King, Junior. You don't get things your way. That's your number and you can't change it. From now on, when you call in just give your number and that's it," JT laid down the law again.

"Uh, okay, will do, 36 it is," I responded, acquiescing.

After the first week, the training program became more intensive. I would attend training five days a week at different locations. On a typical day, I would call JT at exactly my designated time and receive my orders for the day, then meet in a hotel room, a conference room, parking lot, park, gun range, or some other specified place. The locations would vary from day to day. Generally, on Monday and Wednesday mornings I would receive training in surveillance and counter-surveillance techniques. After lunch, I would go to the gym and receive martial arts training. On Tuesday and Thursday mornings, I would receive training in policy and procedures, and in the afternoons I would attend firearms, narcotics, and explosive recognition training. The training was long and a bit lonely, but I loved it all the same.

Fridays

After a long week of training I looked forward to Fridays because typically my only responsibility would be to call JT and then I would start my three-day weekend.

0900 – *ring, ring, ring.*

"JT's tamales," a familiar voice answered.

"Three-six ringing in, have a great weekend," I said.

"Three-six, today is a work day. Sam will meet you at 1000 hours. At Sherman Way and Sepulveda, you will see a credit union on the southeast corner. Just park and wait at the bus bench on the east side. Sam will meet you there," JT said in an all business tone.

"So, no three-day weekend, sir," I replied.

"Three-six, quit using the word sir. Only cops or military use that word." His voice had hardened, telling me he was in full-work mode.

"Okay, I'll do my best," I responded.

"Now get your ass moving," JT said as he hung up the phone.

I drove to the location, parked and walked to the bus bench. I was sitting there for about five minutes thinking about how I'd never ridden on a public bus before, nor had I ever sat at a bus bench. We'd always had a car and no need for public transportation. Just then, Samantha walked up behind me and tapped me on the shoulder. She just smiled, but didn't say anything and began to walk away.

I stood up and followed the scent of her perfume, feeling underdressed in my shorts, T-shirt, and tennis shoes. Her black pencil skirt hugged her body and a white blouse fell off her shoulder, exposing her skin. Her skin looked flawless as she turned and waited for me.

We began to walk towards a high-rise building on the east side of Sepulveda. As I looked at her I thought there was something different about her today, a definite sense of confidence or swag about her that I hadn't noticed before, but we still didn't speak. As we entered the glass building, Samantha reached down and grabbed my hand. Shocked, instinctually, my hand pulled away from hers, but she tightened her grip.

My head turned towards her but she didn't return my look as we entered a small doctor's office.

"Good morning. We have an appointment with Dr. Stevens at 1030," she said with a huge smile to the girl at the front reception desk.

"Mr. and Mrs. Boyd?" the receptionist asked while looking at a computer screen.

"Yes, ma'am," Samantha replied.

"Thank you, please have a seat and the doctor will call you when she's ready," the receptionist confirmed.

Samantha continued to hold my hand as we turned and took seats in the lobby. Our hands separated.

"Samantha, what is going on," I whispered. She bowed her head and started to cry. I looked around, confused. A woman sitting across from us got up and carried over a tissue.

"Are you okay? Would you like a tissue," the lady asked as she put her hand on Samantha's shoulder to console her. The woman looked at me with a scowl.

"Thank you, I'm fine. I'll be fine. Thank you," Samantha sobbed. The door opens. "Mr. and Mrs. Boyd?"

Samantha stood up, and I followed her. She patted her eye with the tissue the woman had just given her, as I looked to see if she had real tears on her face.

"Good morning you two, follow me please." We followed what I assumed was a doctor, I wasn't sure what type, down a long hallway. I went to grab Samantha's hand to console her, but she pushed it away.

The doctor entered a small ten-by-ten room. The room was cold. The carpet was dated and the walls were painted canary yellow. A rocking chair with a worn pad faced a couch resting against the wall. A desk and another small chair sat against the other wall. I quickly scanned the walls and observed several educational degrees in red oak frames. Bachelors, Doctorate of Psychology.

"Well, you look like an attractive healthy couple and I'm glad you took the first step to make your marriage better. What can I do for you two today?" the doctor asked. "Lisa, would you like to start?"

Silence filled the room as the tension rose and my hands began to sweat.

Lisa? Who the fuck is Lisa...what the hell is going on? my inner voice was screaming.

"Okay, Steve, why don't you start? Is it Steve or Steven?" the doctor asked me.

I quickly looked at Samantha, but she didn't look back at me.

"It's okay, I'll start. It's mainly me, not Steven," Samantha – or the Lisa she was pretending to be – said. "We have only been married two years now and things have changed. I don't feel like we're close anymore. I'm alone a lot because Steven is always working and I don't feel special or loved anymore."

"How long have you been feeling like this, Lisa?" asked the shrink.

"About three months now. I don't know. He's just not affectionate anymore." Samantha's head dropped slightly with her response as she started to sob again.

"Steve, is that true?" the shrink asked, now focusing on me.

"I don't think so," I said without much certainty.

"Do you tell Lisa that you love her?" The shrink tilted her head sideways and stared at me after delivering her question.

Samantha quickly responded, "No, he doesn't tell me that he loves me anymore."

"Do you guys still kiss?" the shrink asked Lisa. "You know, there are studies out there where researchers can tell a lot about a marriage based on the frequency couples kiss," the shrink explained. "Let's start off with this questionnaire first, then we will do an exercise which will tell me a lot about you two so we can start to bring you back to being a loving couple. Okay?" The shrink handed both Samantha and I clipboards. A three-page questionnaire was attached; Samantha started filling hers out as I looked at her, then back at my questionnaire.

"All finished, great!" the shrink said, taking our paperwork when we were finished. "Now, I want you two to do this exercise. Lisa, I want you to look into Steven's eyes and tell him from your heart what you love about him," the shrink explained.

Inside I couldn't figure out if they were just fucking with me again or if this was a real shrink, in a real shrink's office. Should I go along with this or not? I was completely out of my element and I was not prepared.

Samantha (Lisa) turned towards me and reached out and grabbed both of my sweaty hands. Her leg touched mine as she turned to face me. She pulled both of my hands towards her and they landed on her skirt. A warm brush of air hit my sweaty palms.

"Steven, I love your laugh, your smile, your kind spirit, your work ethic and your faith in God. I love that you take care of me. You are the love of my life and my best friend. I love you with all of my heart," Lisa said as she stared deeply into my eyes, never wavering. My heart raced and I could feel my ears getting warm.

"Great job, Lisa. Now Steven, it's your turn," the shrink said to me.

"Lisa…" My voice cracked.

"Steven, please look into her eyes when you talk to her," the shrink scolded me.

"Lisa, I like your smile and your… heart. You have a good heart. Yes… you have a great heart. You're funny… You're hot and definitely courageous," I said as I cracked a smile.

"See, he thinks everything is a joke!" Lisa exclaimed to the shrink.

"Okay, Steven… Good, that's a great start." The shrink was praising me, I thought.

"Tell you what, guys, let's try this, because men typically have more difficulty expressing their feelings. Let's try this exercise," the shrink explained. "Now, what I would like you to do is kiss your wife for three seconds and show her how much you love her."

My head turned to Samantha then quickly back to the shrink and my eyes widened. *I need to stop this don't I? I think Samantha is married, and I have a girlfriend. This is crazy.* I felt Samantha squeeze my hand hard, so I turned back towards her. Our eyes locked on each other's and she began to lean towards me. I started to turn my head slightly to the right as I met her in the middle. Our lips touched and I watched her close her eyes. Her lips were soft and full. Her grip on my hands softened and I felt her tongue enter my mouth. I reciprocated as our tongues slowly met. After what seemed like a lifetime, she pulled away. "I love you Steven," she said.

"You do? I mean, I love you too." I stumbled over my words as I continued to process what was going on.

"Great job, guys! That's all for our first session but here's some homework for you two and I'll see you next week," the shrink said with a smile.

Samantha popped to her feet, gave the shrink a hug and told her, "Thank you, doctor. I was scared to come here, but I really think this will help us. We'll see you next week."

"Steven, are you coming next week?" the shrink asked me.

There was a pause because I was still thinking about our kiss and trying to figure out what had just happened. I finally managed to respond, "Oh, okay. Bye, Doc."

Samantha extended her hand out to mine; we clasped hands as we left the office. She didn't say a word as we walked towards the door. I kept looking at her, but her head was fixed and focused as her pace quickened. As we exited the building she immediately tossed my hand away.

"Report to the usual location on Monday at 1000," she said in an unemotional voice, then turned towards her car.

As she continued to walk away, I asked, "Samantha, what is going on?"

"It's Sam… I go by Sam," she said as she kept walking towards her car.

"What?" I asked, still trying to figure out what the hell was going on.

Sam turned back, revealing a slight smile on her face. "Today's Friday! Fridays are test days, silly."

"Test days? What the hell? Really?"

"Exactly, welcome to the program. You're too nice for this job, Mac. Get out while you can. I don't think you're cut out for it. You did terribly," she said as she walked away with that same grin, then turned back, "except for the kiss." She chuckled as she walked away.

Training Module No. 2

Monday – I showed up at the usual location and waited for my signal.

Beep, beep, beep. My pager went off. "234-1015," came across the display. Room 234 at 1015 hours. Like I was trained, I took the stairs up to the second floor ensuring I wasn't being followed.

JT answered the door. As I walked in, I saw Jack, David, and Sam sitting at a small table inside the hotel room.

"Come in and take a seat," said JT. David stepped up and shook my hand. JT continued, "Today is going to be a very important day for you. You've made it through the first part of your training. We're going to fill you in on some behind the curtain stuff on the program and tell you how it works."

David went on to explain, "Me, JT, Sam, Jayson, and Jack are in charge of selecting the birds and training them. A bird is what we call an undercover officer if you haven't figured that out yet. After you're trained, we pass you off to your handlers. Your handlers are detectives that investigate certain terrorist groups. After training, you will only see us for quarterly training updates or department administrative duties. All your contact will be with your handlers and not with us after training. Do you understand?"

"I do. Who are my handlers or when does that happen?"

"You have already met them. Do you remember Albert and Claire from your interview?" asked Jack.

I knew exactly who they were. I especially remembered Albert. He was the guy with the *resting dick* face. I began to get a little worried, but I went with it. "Sure, I remember them," I said, nodding my head.

"Cool! They are your handlers and you will be with them starting next week, just for one day a week. The other days you are still with us," David explained.

"So I'll train with both of you?" I asked.

"Yes, but for different types of training; they will be responsible for training you on your group's ideology and background, but that's about it. We will still train you on how to be an undercover officer and how not to get killed," JT said.

"Okay. What group am I assigned to?" I asked.

"Actually, the training unit won't know, we will never know, and we don't want to know anything about your group. It's just cleaner that way," Jack stated.

"I don't believe that. You really expect me to believe you don't know my group? Just go ahead and give me the need to know, right to know line."

"Seriously, Drew!" JT said, raising his voice. It was the first time they had called me by my name in more than a month. "We don't know, and you are not to tell anyone who your group is and that includes us. Am I clear on that? You tell no one, including us!" JT reaffirmed.

JT went on to tell me that I had successfully completed the first half of the training in record time. Over the next few weeks I would switch to a different set of training blocks. On Mondays and Wednesdays, I'd learn human behavior, interview and interrogation techniques and survival skills. Tuesdays and Thursdays I'd learn observation and listening skills in the mornings and electronic surveillance in the afternoons.

2130 hours – Ring, ring, ring… The caller ID was blocked so I didn't answer. Ring, ring, ring… Still no caller ID so I let it go to voicemail but they didn't leave a message.

Beep, beep, beep… "932-2222." The 932 was Sam's call sign and the 2222 was call her Code 2, which meant it was a priority, but not an emergency. My heart started to race and my palms began to sweat ever so slightly. I picked up the phone and gave her a call.

"Steven, it's Lisa. Meet me at the Sandlot in fifteen." It was Sam's voice, but she was referring to herself by her undercover name, Lisa. She sounded panicked, maybe; I couldn't be sure.

"Lisa, it's 9:30 at night, is everything okay?" I said, fishing for information to assess.

"See you in fifteen," she responded, then hung up.

I jumped in the shower, swigged some mouthwash and ran out the door to the Sandlot. I walked into the bar, but I didn't see Sam. I sat in the lobby waiting for her, but she wasn't there. After fifteen minutes, I paged her.

Beep, beep…

I turned, expecting to see Sam, but heard Jack's voice. "Hey Steven, you buying tonight?" My head dropped and I felt like I'd screwed up again, but didn't know how. We walked to the bar and sat down.

"Steve, we had you from the time you left your house. You didn't check your mirrors; you took a direct route here and you didn't dry clean yourself. You walked into the bar and you didn't do anything we taught you. As a matter of fact, you did the complete opposite and sat in the lobby, right where God and Country can see you during a sensitive meet. Not even a simple disguise? Do you have a death wish, son?" He's begun to raise his voice at me, which comes natural because we just don't care for each other.

"If you don't think what we are teaching you is for real and can save your life someday, then it's time for you to leave. If you just had your head up your ass, then don't let it happen again. Or maybe you were just thinking with your dick, which will leave you dead, broke, or both. Don't ever forget that! Thanks for the beer, kid," Jack said as he downed it, slapped me on my back harder than normal, and walked out.

I took a swallow of my beer and placed the frosted mug down on the counter top trying to identify which of my feelings and emotions were the greatest. As I felt defeated and was wondering if I truly wanted or could do this job, a piece of ice slid down the mug onto the bar. The piece of ice settled on the bar, leaving a trail of water behind. Suddenly, a familiar smell appeared at my left shoulder and I felt an energy directly behind me; I didn't look, nor did I break my concentration on the piece of ice, now melting on the counter top.

"Steven, it's not that bad," a female voice whispered in my ear. I didn't answer. "May I sit?" she asked.

"Suit yourself," I responded, continuing to stare at the now-melted piece of ice.

"Hey, I'm sorry about that," Sam whispered as she leaned in. There was a long pause. "It was for your own good, you know that, right?"

"If you say so. What shall I call you tonight?" I inquired, still not making eye contact.

"What do you want to call me?" Sam responded in a flirtatious voice.

"Bitch sounds pretty good right now," I said as I raised my head and locked eyes with her with a scowl on my face.

"Steven, I'm going to teach you a lot tonight, but first you need to buy me a drink." Her head tossed from left to right and then back down so she was looking at the counter.

"Is that right? I don't think so, Sam... Lisa... or whoever you are. I think I've learned enough for one night and I'm not in the mood." I finished my beer and asked for the check.

Sam stood up and whispered in my ear, "Drew, no bullshit, this is where you need to grow as a bird. Stay, let me help you. Please, just sit." She grabbed my hand. Her scent began to soften me; we sat and she placed her hand on my thigh.

"I'm tired of this shit! I'm tired of these games. I don't know what I'm doing or who I'm supposed to be, where and when I'm supposed to be somebody else... never knowing who... and all I hear from you guys is how I've fucked up again."

"Drew, just stay with me. You're doing great, but they'll never tell you that. It's all just a test to see if you'll quit, don't you see that? Just like in the academy," Sam explained.

My mind raced with confusing thoughts, but I decided to hear her out. "Bartender, I'll take another beer and she will have..."

Sam cut me off. "Scotch please, neat." Sam began to talk, "Drew, emotions will get you killed in this business. Emotions cannot affect your decision-making. Emotions are your enemy. They will either expose you or get you killed. You have to learn how to control your emotions and sometimes the easiest way to do that is to block them. Tonight when I paged you Code 2 that brought certain emotions to you which blocked your rational decision-making, your ability to look at the big picture of the scenario and apply what you have learned. I exploited one of your weaknesses."

"What weakness was that? I don't have any weaknesses!"

"What went through your mind when I paged you Code 2? Think about it. Really think about it and be honest."

"You paged me Code 2 so I thought you were in trouble. You've never paged me like that before."

"Okay, and when we spoke, what did you think then?"

"I didn't think of anything except I thought you might be in trouble," I responded, starting to get frustrated with the conversation.

"Okay, if that's true then why did you shower first?" She tilted her head and grinned.

"Showered? You know that I showered?" More games? I shook my head and took another drink.

"Drew, let's face it. If you really believed I was in trouble would you have showered first? I think you thought that I was calling you for a booty call." She was looking at me intensely. She continued, "It doesn't matter which one you were thinking because they are both an effective tool that you need to learn how you can use or when it's being used against you. Do you understand what I'm telling you?" Her smile faded as she looked directly into my eyes.

"Let me get this straight. You think that when I saw your page that I thought it was a booty call? Did I get that right?"

Sam grabbed her drink, "Of course you did! You're a guy, and let's face it, I have great tits and a nice ass."

As I processed what she was saying, I took a drink of my beer and scanned her body.

"Drew, quit thinking about fucking me right now…"

"I'm not…"

"Drew, shut up for one minute and listen to me." She nudged me with her shoulder. "I'm trying to teach you something. It doesn't matter which emotion you felt, either you were thinking I needed help or the excitement of the unknown. It doesn't matter, they both work. I was able to place your emotions at the top of your mind by a simple page, late at night, which caused you to forget all the safety measures we trained you in and what your mission was. You ran out the door like a dog in heat, forgot two months' worth of training and I didn't even have to get naked or give you a blow job. Do you see that?"

I didn't respond.

"Do you understand?" Sam asked again.

"You played me?" I said, starting to realize the full scope of her deviousness.

"Of course I did," she exclaimed. "That's what we do. Play people, manipulate situations to our advantage so we can gather intelligence without anyone knowing we're doing it; or if you're good, they don't even know you were there. If you understand that and can recognize that, and even better, master it, you'll be effective and you'll stay alive!"

"That feels wrong to me. Is that not wrong?"

"How is it wrong?" She started to crack a smile as I heard her mutter, "I knew you were too nice for this." Her body shifted back away from me as she took a drink of scotch. "Mac," she turned her head toward me now and her hair covered half of her face. "It's not against the law. Men and women do it to each other every day, but their motivations are different. Parents do it to their children too, and that's not wrong. In this case, you're an undercover cop, and you're doing it to save lives. I think that's more important and I definitely don't see it as wrong." She stopped making her case and took another sip of scotch.

"I get it... but I don't know how to do it and I'm not sure I want to." My head dropped and I took another drink.

"Drew, you have a natural ability to read people and situations. Better than any bird I've seen come through this program. Focus on your goal or target person first, find out what makes them tick, what's important to them, what motivates them, better yet, what's most important to them, then work backwards." She put her drink down and turned toward me.

"What do you mean?" I asked.

"We'll show you, but not tonight." She took another drink.

"Why not tonight? Why are things always on your time and not mine?" I can hear my voice rising with frustration.

"That's exactly why! Your ego has to go. That macho thing will get you killed or exposed here. I don't know if you have something to prove or you have little-man syndrome... or whatever it is going on in your head, but you have to let it go. Ego in the undercover world is like kryptonite to Superman," Sam rambled.

"You like Superman?" My head lifted with intrigue. "You know he's the all-time best superhero, right?"

"Seriously! You're always messing around," she said in frustration as I cracked a smile and took another drink of my beer. She shook her head with frustration.

"I don't have an ego, either," I stated.

"That is your ego saying that! Can't you see that? Most guys I know with huge egos either have something to prove or a small penis, so which is it?" She began to laugh as she gazed down at my crotch.

"I don't have anything to prove, so I guess that leaves a small penis. And all these years I thought I was good down there," I answered sarcastically, shifting my body toward hers.

"Can you say EGO?" she smiled and shook her head. "Shut up, learn to listen, and drop the ego… Walk me out, I have to go. I have a date." Sam shot the remainder of her scotch without hesitation.

"You have a date? I thought you were married."

"Nope, what made you think that?"

"Your wedding ring…" I said, the obvious answer.

"Wow, oh my, you poor thing." Sam chuckled… Both of us realizing how stupid my statement was in the company I was in.

As I walked Sam to her car, she asked me, "So which was it?"

"What's that?" I asked.

"Don't play stupid with me. Did you think I was in trouble or that I wanted a booty call?" She smiled while asking.

"I thought you needed help of course," I said, remembering my ego lesson.

"Wrong again, Steven. You're not very good at this are you?" She smiled and got into her car.

Training Module No. 3

I was accelerating in the training program and knew JT was pleased with my progress. The operational side of the training came easy to me. I had trained in martial arts for years and wrestled in high school, the electronic surveillance was fascinating; and the firearms and explosive training was challenging, but cool. I was getting paid to learn how to shoot and blow things up. The disguise stuff was different and not really my thing, but looking back on it came in very handy some days. The two remaining training topics were my observation skills and my interview and interrogation skills. Over the next few weeks, most of my training focused on those two areas.

I was meeting Jayson at a park in the Los Angeles area one day. I arrived early and saw him approaching me from the west.

"Junior, how are you? Are you ready to learn today?" Jayson asked me.

"Sure, let's do it," I said, feeling confident. I liked Jayson and was glad I wasn't with the *Adam Henry*, i.e. Jack.

"What do you think the difference between *listening* and *hearing* are?" Jayson asked.

"The spelling?" I started to laugh, but Jayson didn't seem to think it was funny. "I don't know where you're going with this, Jayson," I added, trying to recover.

"Well, it's a very important skill you need to learn. It's essential for this assignment and you'll definitely need it with your future wife. There is hearing someone and listening to someone, but they are very different. Most people listen because it comes naturally, but they don't actually *hear* people."

"What do you mean?"

"Well, everyone listens. Just as you are listening to me, but you haven't learned to hear me yet. Listening is the audible part, but hearing is understanding the true meaning of what someone is saying."

"Okay, I think I know what you're saying."

"Let me show you." Jayson's head turned left as he began to scan the park. There was a woman walking a dog on the sidewalk to the north; two women posing in the downward dog yoga position in the grassy area immediately to the south, and an older gentleman sitting on the curb of the playground keeping a watchful eye on two small children on the play set.

"Follow me," Jayson said as we walked towards the play set and the older gentleman.

Jayson said, "Excuse me, sir?" The man turned his head toward us, but didn't say anything.

"Excuse me, sir, sorry to bother you, but did you happen to see a dog wander through here?" Jayson asked the man.

"No, sir, we haven't and we've been here… since 1:30," the man mumbled as he tried to figure out what time he arrived. "I picked my grandkids up from school at noon then we drove over here from Bishop

Street, so we've been here for about an hour and we haven't seen any dogs run through, sorry. Is the dog chipped?"

Jayson responded, "Yes, sir, he is, so if you happen to see him just call the pound and they'll call me."

"Yes sir, I will, but I would suggest you fix your fence too," the man offered.

"Good point. Thank you, have a nice day," Jayson said as we walked away. "So, what did you hear?" Jayson asked me.

"I heard him say that he hadn't seen our dog and he thinks our dog is a she instead of a he."

"Here is what I heard. He's a grandpa who watches his daughter's two kids on a regular basis. The kids go to a pre-school on Bishop Street about twenty minutes away from here. He lives within walking distance of the park and is most likely widowed or not married anymore. He is, or once was, a dog owner and the dog was most likely a female. He thinks I am negligent for allowing my dog to continue to escape and he hasn't seen our dog. That's what I heard. Do you see the difference?"

"Wow, I didn't hear it that way, but now looking back you are exactly right. I see it now," I responded in amazement.

Jayson and I went back over to the picnic tables and Jayson said, "Don't look, but a kid's train passes behind you every five minutes. I want you to tell me how many cars make up the train."

"Okay, but I'm not allowed to look? How can I do that?"

"Think big picture. Think outside the box. Figure it out… Take your time. There are several ways to do it, if you allow your brain to think outside of the way society has conditioned it to think you will find a way," Jayson said with confidence.

I heard the whistle of the train blow as it got closer. Clack, clack… Clack, clack… Clack, clack… Clack, clack… Clack, clack… then the clacks went silent. "Jayson, there are five cars on that train."

"Good, how did you do it?"

"I counted the clacks of the carts and figured there was one cart for every two clacks."

"Great job," he said, beginning to smile. "Can you give me another way?"

I looked at him and realized that there was a reflection in his *Top Gun*-style glasses.

"I now see the reflection in your glasses, but I just noticed it and I should be able to see the cars as they go by," I responded with a feeling of true learning and confidence.

"Perfect! Do you know another way?"

"Really, there are more ways?"

"Of course there are! Remember, never limit yourself, or the possibilities," he said as he continued to challenge the traditional thinking methods that had been embedded in my mind. I looked around, trying to find another solution, when I saw that the two women who had previously been in the downward dog position had completed their workouts and were walking towards us.

"Excuse me ladies, can you be the tie-breaker to a little wager my grandpa and I are having?" I asked the woman.

"Who, us?" They looked bewildered as they answered.

"Don't worry, it's a simple one. If I were to ask you how many cars are attached to the train coming behind me what would your answer be, including the caboose?" I asked.

The train whistle blew as the clacking came into earshot. Humorously (at least to me), both began to count out loud, "One, two, three, four, five. There are five," they both yelled out with excitement.

"Who said five?" the more attractive woman asked.

"Grandpa, you're right again! Thank you, ladies, you have a great day."

The women walked off and I felt a sense of accomplishment.

"Grandpa? FU, kid," Jayson started to laugh. "Excellent, we're done for today. Great job. Remember to think outside of the box and deprogram yourself from how society and the police department have brain-washed you into thinking and gathering information. Do you realize, Drew, you found three ways to gather a piece of intelligence about the train, without ever looking at it? No one would ever suspect you as the one who got the info, right, because you never looked at the train. Can you see where this applies to undercover work now?"

"I can… I actually can. I think I finally get it, because I never really thought of it that way," I answered proudly.

"You see, our minds are our weapons… our thought processes and words are our tactics. Always think tactical…" Jayson explained as he put his hand on my shoulder. "Now let's go get a hot dog. They have the best hot dogs here." He began to walk towards a little hole-in-the-wall hot dog cart in the park.

"Really?"

"No, not really… but let's get one anyway," Jayson said and we both laughed.

New Name…

MacGregor, anxious and nervous to find out his new identity and assignment, anticipated the meeting with uncertainty.   Beep, beep, beep. The pager read 325-1245. I looked at my watch – I had an hour to kill before 1245, but knew I was close to the Glendale Hotel so I decided to get something to eat first. As I finished the last of my double/double (no tomatoes or onions, add pickles) I noticed a tan Toyota Camry to the west. I got into my truck and started my counter-surveillance techniques before heading to the meet-up location.

The Camry stayed parked at the curb, but I saw a man pick up a radio as I passed his vehicle. I stayed in the number one lane and set up to make a left turn; I saw the point of a very poorly executed surveillance team, blue Honda, in the number two lane. I was pissed that these guys were tailing me again, on such an important day.

Protocols were to abort the meet if I knew I was being tailed, but I didn't want to.

"Screw this. I'm going to lose this tail," I said out loud to myself.

I drove in the opposite direction of my meet location towards a multi-leveled shopping mall, knowing that once I entered the underground parking structure, I'd turn the table in my favor and it would be tough for the surveillance team to follow me.

Typically, police radios won't work in an underground parking structure; air support, the mighty eye from the sky, is eliminated; the team would be forced to put out a *foot man* if they were to have any chance of finding me, leaving the team short and exposed.

I parked my car on the bottom level and grabbed my backpack as I walked into the mall. I looked at my watch: 1215 hours. I had thirty minutes to get to room 325 for the meet; I could still make it. I hurried to the first men's restroom that I saw, quickly changing clothes and adding a hat with a long wig that I had stashed in my backpack. A quick switch and I was on foot, making my way across the street to the bus stop. I was in luck – I saw a shuttle stop for the local hotels. I jumped on the shuttle and with nine minutes to spare I arrived at the hotel. I ran up the stairs to the second floor where I changed back into my clothes and walked up to the third floor, ensuring I didn't have a tail.

1245 Hours

Albert opened the door.

"Hey," I said.

Albert looked surprised. "You're here? How did you get here?"

"What do you mean?" I responded as I saw Claire sitting at the desk next to the two double beds. "You paged me. We have a meeting at 1245, right?" I said, closing the door behind me.

"Yes, hold on. I'll be right back." Albert left, looking flustered.

"Is everything okay?" I asked Claire. She started to smile.

"You're good. They told him you were at the mall right now, but don't tell Albert I told you. Nobody's ever done that to Albert before." Claire continued to grin.

"I'm not at the mall and I'm definitely not a nobody. So, are we going to do this meeting or were you guys just fucking with me again?" I asked her undeservingly, with a pissed-off tone.

"Let's wait for Albert to get back and see what he wants to do. This is going to be good," Claire chuckled.

Albert returned to the room about ten minutes later as Claire and I were engaged in small talk.

"Take a seat… Three-Six, do you know what the protocols are when you spot a tail?" Albert barked at me.

"Of course I do," I replied.

"So why are you here then? You obviously spotted the tail. Is that right?"

"I did."

"So why the fuck are you here then?" Albert's face had started to turn red as his emotions began to cloud his reasoning.

"I'm here because we had a meeting and you're supposed to tell me my new identity and group," I calmly replied, infuriating Albert even more.

"That's not what I'm talking about and you know it. If you spot a tail, you're supposed to abort the meet and you didn't do it. Your ego keeps getting in the way, and in this case, you could have gotten us all killed if this was real."

I shook my head. "Albert, the protocols say abort the mission if you're being tailed. I wasn't being tailed anymore. I lost my tail using the training I was taught and that's why I am here. My ego is in check. Why are you so pissed, because I burned your tail? You would think you

117

would be proud of me because I'm here on time using everything I was taught," I argued.

"Who the fuck do you think you're talking to, kid! You violated a major safety protocol!"

"Hey, that line is from *Top Gun*, isn't it? That's my favorite movie," I responded, but it came across very sarcastically.

Albert cut my rambling off. "What the fuck are you talking about? Here I am trying to have a serious conversation and you're just fucking around."

"Oh, I'm sorry about that. I didn't mean any disrespect, I promise, but I didn't violate anything," I explained.

Albert continued wanting to argue his position but I remembered my training about emotionally charged arguments. It was clear to me for the first time that I had Albert in the palm of my hand.

I continued, "Albert, I can see that you are very emotional so why don't we agree to disagree on this?" I could see the anger as Albert's muscles visibly tensed. "Just call JT and let me know because I did exactly what I was trained to do," I said, continuing to push Albert's buttons. "You guys figure it out and let me know," I said.

Claire chimed in, "Three-Six, why don't you just take the rest of the day off and we'll figure this out and get back to you tomorrow?"

"Sounds good, Claire, just let me know. Albert, my apologies again. I was just doing what I was trained to do." I turned to leave. I was really beginning to understand how to think outside of the box, changing my thinking, and understanding how to manipulate emotions to gain information.

Later that night, I received several phone calls regarding the incident and for the first time I saw a division between the training unit and the handlers. I wasn't privy to what occurred between the two sections and I really didn't care, but I was told they had agreed to disagree. The next day I met with Claire and Albert again. This time there were no tails, no pager message, no drama; just a phone call. "Drew, meet me and Claire at the hotel at 1100. I will page you the room number when I get it," Albert said in a professional voice.

"Sounds good, Albert," I responded, all business today.

As I walked into the room, Claire was sitting in the usual place and Albert was surprisingly jovial and friendly to me.

"Today is a big day for you. I know you have been waiting for this day. Are you ready?" he asked.

"Yes, I believe I am," I told him.

"Here is your name: Steven Mathews. You were born on October 7th, 1970 in Newport, Rhode Island. Your mother's name is Kimberly O'Brien, and your dad's name is Barron Mathews. Your father was a Lieutenant Colonel in the Navy and your parents were never married; your father was killed when you were young, and the last you had heard your mother lived in New York somewhere. These are the 'nuts and bolts' of your new life. The rest of your life and background you will create. You will actually write it out and create it yourself so you can remember it. Does that make sense to you?" Albert asked.

"Kind of," I said, nodding my head in agreement.

"What do you think of your new name?" Claire asked in an extra high-pitched voice.

"I'm not too crazy about Steven, but it makes sense to me now because that's what Sam has been calling me for the last three months. Can I go by Steve?"

"It doesn't matter as long as it fits in your background. JT and his crew will guide you." Claire said.

"Okay, I thought JT's crew didn't know or weren't allowed to know my name? That's what he told me."

"His crew knows your name, but they won't know your group and if you tell them you will be done in this program, do you hear me! I don't want that son-of-a-bitch messing with my case. Don't tell him or any of his goons, understood?" Al was pissed, confirming my suspicions about the disconnect between the two sections.

"I won't. What group will I be assigned to?" I asked.

"You are assigned to the *White Power* side, they are kind of dead right now, but we have seen a spike of action in the Orange County area," Albert responded.

"White Power. Oh, wow. I don't know if I can do that or not. Those guys are crazy," I responded, feeling nervous suddenly.

"You'll be fine, don't worry. Starting tomorrow you will start to receive ideology training on White Power. What they believe, how they dress, where they hang out, etc. You need to know it and build it into your background. You will train five days a week now, two with us and three with JT and his crew. On Mondays and Wednesdays, you now report to me and Claire and you don't need to check in with JT and his crew on those days. The other days you report to JT as usual," Albert explained.

"Okay, how much longer is my training or when does all of this start?" I asked.

"I want everything done and you moved out by June," Albert said.

"You want me moved out within two months? Wow, that's fast. When will I find out if I passed training then?" I inquired, still unsure where I stood in the program.

"What are you talking about? You passed training a long time ago, Drew. You will be out of here by June if I have my way," Albert responded, frustrated with what he'd clearly interpreted as a stupid question.

Training Module No. 4

Most of my training now consisted of small tasks or missions. JT and the crew sent me out to different locations to practice my undercover skills, but they were pretty simple. They sent me to bars or restaurants with specific targets and objectives. My missions consisted of successfully identifying my target and getting the required information as briefed to me prior to each mission. The target might be an unsuspecting waitress at the local Denny's, a bank teller, or a policeman. At one point, I had three missions going on at the same time. On most missions, I would get the information requested within the first contact or second for sure. There was only one mission that was giving me trouble – Lupe. I was told that she worked at a coffee shop in Pasadena. My mission was simple, to find out the following:

1. Phone number

2. Address

3. Vehicles

4. As many friends, family or associate's names as possible

I located her at the coffee shop very easily but she was much more attractive than in the picture I had been given. I had made contact with her on two previous occasions and found out her work schedule from a co-worker, but she wouldn't give me the time of day. On this particular day, it was a Tuesday; she must have gotten up early because her hair and make-up were done, and she wore a soft perfume that I had never noticed before. She saw me come into the shop and I sat at my usual table. When the line died down, she walked over to my table, bringing my usual hot chocolate.

"Steven, how are you today? Here's your hot chocolate with no whip, right?" she asked me.

"Hi Lupe, you look great today. I love your hair," I said, acknowledging the extra effort she'd probably put into it.

"So, what are you saying, that I normally look like crap?" she said with a thick accent and a smile that caught me off guard.

"No, no, not at all. I didn't mean that… You know that, right? I've been coming in here for weeks now just trying to get the nerve up to ask you to dinner," I responded, attempting to recover from my previous statement.

"What, Oh really. Umm…" Lupe was visibly shaken by my directness.

"So, what do you think? Dinner?" I waited for her response.

"Umm, can I let you know later? I'm sorry," she said, walking away.

She was obviously flustered and somewhat unnatural. Was she married or did she have a boyfriend? I hadn't observed a wedding ring but I had definitely learned that didn't provide much accurate information.

Lupe returned about fifteen minutes later with a chain of events worked out. "How about tonight, Steve? I'll pick you up at 4:00. Will that work?"

"You'll pick me up? I can pick you up, it's okay," I responded, thinking it was odd she wanted to pick me up.

"No, I'd rather pick you up, and sorry it's so early, but I have plans later tonight so it's just dinner." Lupe looked for my acceptance and understanding that we were just going to dinner and that was it.

"Okay, sounds good. I'll be at the gym playing racquetball if you want to pick me up there or just tell me where and I'll meet you there," I responded, because I didn't want her to know where I lived, just as I'd been trained.

"No, it's okay. I'll pick you up at the gym at 4:00," Lupe said.

"It's a date. Can I at least plan the date or do you want to do that too?" I asked, in a teasing tone.

"No, it's dinner and it's a surprise. Wear something casual and you won't need a coat," Lupe said, confirming she was in charge.

"Great, see you then," I responded, but felt that something wasn't right. I just couldn't figure out what it was. The whole situation seemed strange to me. Lupe seemed nervous when she returned, but it wasn't

125

like first date butterflies. Never had a girl wanted to go to dinner at 4:00 and insisted on driving. Perplexing… and she'd told me not to wear a coat. Very strange. I still didn't know her last name, address, or phone number. I wasn't sure what I should do. Call JT and ask? Was I just overthinking this thing? Lupe was a beautiful girl who worked at a coffee shop and I was the one who had asked her out, right?

Four o'clock came around and I saw her pull up into the lot in a gold Honda Accord, license plate number 3TYI253 with current December tags. The windows were blacked out. The car didn't fit her. Watching from the front of the gym, I observed her unbuckle her seat belt as the vehicle slowed and I committed the license plate to memory. I scanned the parking lot for *unfriendlies* and peered into her car as she came to a stop. Her work smock was folded neatly on the rear passenger seat.

She rolled down the window. "Hi, Steven are you ready?"

I opened the passenger door to get in and noticed a large dirt footprint on the bottom of the door panel as if it had been kicked. The smell of the car didn't match the type of perfume she normally wore, which typically saturated a girl's car. The front seat carpets were stained heavily, but the back-seat carpet appeared new.

"It's good to see you. Thanks for picking me up. Where are we going?" I asked before I entered the car.

"I told you, it's a surprise," Lupe responded, avoiding eye contact.

"Great, I love surprises. Is it close or do we have a drive?" I asked, seeking additional intelligence.

"No, it's not too far, the location is about fifteen minutes away," she said.

She just said 'location', I thought. What girl says 'location'? Damn it, Drew, you have been set up again, she's a cop...

The December registration tags – all police vehicles were registered in December. The footprint on the door panel – cops are notoriously lazy and tend to kick the door panel to close the door. The stained front carpets and clean back seat carpets. The blacked-out windows. The unbuckling of her seatbelt prior to coming to a stop. The unfamiliarity of the car. This was an old surveillance car and she had to be a cop. That was why there had been a hesitation when I'd asked her out. She probably went and called her supervisor looking for direction. No wonder I hadn't been able to crack this girl...

I need to abort this mission now, I thought to myself. *There is nothing good that is going to come out of this*, but then I thought, *No. I am going to do this. It's training, right. Let's see where this goes…* Sam's ego speech popped into my head, yelling, *abort, abort, abort!* But I knew I was under control, my emotions were in check, and there was no ego here. *Let's see what happens.*

"You're awfully quiet, are you okay?" Lupe asked as I pondered my checklist.

"Oh, sorry about that. I'm fine. So, tell me, Lupe, where are you from?"

"I'm not from around here," she answered evasively.

"Me neither, where are you from?" I pressed on, as I plotted my outs.

"I'm from the South." Another non-descript evasive answer.

"Very cool, a southern girl. But, I don't hear a southern accent from you?"

"No, I wasn't there very long." Her head tilted downward and away as she shifted her body weight in her seat. Her non-verbal signs were telling me she was lying and uncomfortable.

"Where did you grow up?" I continued to make conversation – or question her; however one would interpret it.

"It's called Smalltown, Massachusetts. You've probably never heard of it," she answered, but still didn't look in my direction.

"Wow, what a 'small world,' no pun intended," I started to laugh. "That's so crazy, I *do* know it! Do you know that famous burger joint there in the middle of town called Jerry's? My buddy, Gary and I, actually ate there when we were traveling the East Coast after college." I waited for her response because I had just made up the name Jerry's to see if I could verify my instincts. There was silence. "I'm sure you've eaten there hundreds of times, but it was so cool, we loved it. Did you used to eat there a lot?"

Lupe looked down at the speedometer then into the driver's side mirror, all signs of deception. I saw her blouse begin to rise as her heart beat quickened.

"Yes, I ate there a few times, but I'm not a big fan of burgers," she replied, failing to make eye contact with me. A palpable tension consumed the air in the vehicle.

"Steve, my sister's place is around the corner – do you mind if we stop there first, I have to drop something off really quick and the restaurant is right around the corner," Lupe's voice cracked as she spoke.

"Sure, what's your sister's name?" I asked, now knowing nothing good could come of this stop.

"Drewle," Lupe responded as she negotiated a left turn onto Osborne, using both hands, shuffling the steering wheel from her left to her right without crossing over her wrists; same as I was trained to do in driver's training at the police academy.

"I love that name. Are you guys close?" I asked, checking my "6," but I didn't see a tail. This had to be a fixed-op inside the house. It was the only way that I saw it, and it made the most sense to me. Her job had to be to get me *inside the house.*

"We're besties. Here we are." Lupe initially braked hard as she pulled to the curb in front of 546 North Osborne, smoothing her braking as the car came to a complete stop.

"Okay, I'll stay here," I told her, checking my surroundings.

"No, please come in and meet her. She would kill me if I made you stay in the car," Lupe pleaded.

We both got out of the car and walked towards the front door. I noticed Lupe wasn't carrying anything.

"Lupe, weren't you supposed to drop something off? Do you want me to get it?" I asked her. Lupe looked physically shaken. Her face turned pale. The front door opened and a woman came out. "Hey, sis. This must be Steven."

"Hi Drewle, nice to meet you." I reached out to shake her hand. Her hands were calloused, like a man's.

"Come on in. Do you guys have a minute?" Drewle asked.

"Sure, do you mind?" Lupe turned and motioned for me to step in front of her.

"No, not at all," I replied as we began to walk towards the front door.

Drewle went in first and I followed her through the front door knowing something was waiting for me, but unsure what. As I entered the hose, I looked left and saw a man sitting on the couch. He got up to greet me and I walked towards him. Suddenly, someone placed me in a choke hold from behind. I immediately recognized it, but I was locked in tight and even though I gave my best effort to fend it off, I knew it was over for me. The blood flowing through the carotid arteries in my neck started to slow and my vision slowly went black as I lost consciousness.

A few minutes later, I began to awake, smelling a wooden floor, its coolness on my cheek as I regained consciousness. My vision came into focus next, cloudy, my feet were free, but my wrists had a set of new bracelets restraining them. I scanned the hardwood floor before I attempted to move, but my head was still groggy. I saw through the front window blinds a rescue ambulance parked across the street and a man walking towards the driver. He raised four fingers – code 4; cop lingo for everything is okay – to the south, but I didn't know who he was signaling.

The ambulance left and the man walked out of my view. I heard a side door open as I sat up and scanned the empty room. Then I heard footsteps; I pushed myself up against the nearest wall. The steps were heavy and sounded like a man's – *wait*, I thought, *there's another set* – then another, getting louder. I felt surprisingly calm as I sat against the wall, near the one/two corner of the house waiting for what I was assuming was JT's crew.

"Ahh, three-six, the golden boy, you okay?" JT asked as he entered the room with Jack and Sam. They seemed proud of themselves. Their chests were puffed out as they walked around like peacocks.

"Yeah, I'm fine," I responded.

"I thought we should fuck with you a little more but of course the girl said no," Jack called out as he approached me.

"Are you good? Do you want a drink of water?" Sam asked in a more caring tone.

"Water would be good, thanks," I said as Sam left the room.

"Three-six, what if this was real? What would you do?" Jack asked me with a smirk.

"Not sure, to be honest," I said, as I surveyed my options.

"That's not good enough! This is serious shit and you need to take this seriously. It's your life, not mine," Jack yelled.

"Jack, I never said it wasn't serious… Geez. You've got anger issues," I said under my breath, knowing that I was in control.

"What did you say, asshole?" Jack walked quickly towards me and slapped me upside the head, eliciting the response I might get.

JT jumped up and grabbed him. "Jack, knock that shit off, you hear me!"

Jack walked away and sat in a chair across the room, recognizing that he was clearly out of control.

After Jack slapped me, a slight smirk came across my face because it was clear to us both at that very moment that I had used everything he had taught me about using people's emotions against them.

"Fuck you, Mac," Jack yelled in confirmation.

"Jack, enough, that's an order," JT said calmly.

"Whose house is this?" I asked, but no one answered me. "The Department owns a house outside the city?" Still no response, but they were writing something. "That's pretty wild," I started to chuckle. "Who knew?" I continued to try to get a response. I still couldn't believe these motherfuckers had actually choked me to the point of passing out.

"JT, I told you this kid doesn't get it. He thinks everything is a joke," Jack yelled as he got up from his chair again.

Sam came back into the room with a bottle of water and sensed the tension in the air. "Here's your water. Oh sorry, I forgot you're cuffed. Turn around." Sam reached for her keys.

"Sam, leave them on! This kid isn't getting it," Jack yelled again.

"Jack, relax. He's one of us. He gets it, trust me he gets it," Sam yelled back and pulled out her handcuffs key.

"Sam, I said don't uncuff him." Jack started to walk towards her. He was still physically upset and I actually sensed a little fear in his eyes masked as anger. I slipped one cuff to free my hands, just in case he really wanted to hit me this time, but I kept my hands behind my back, concealing my freedom.

"JT, this is exactly why we don't need women in the unit!" Jack yelled, looking at Sam.

"Jack," JT yelled, then switched to Spanish. Jack stopped walking towards Sam and me and turned around, walking out the front door.

After Jack had left, I reached out to Sam with my right hand, a cuff dangling from my wrist, and grabbed the bottle of water.

"You were free this whole time?" Sam shook her head and sat on a wooden rocking chair across from me. "Do you need a key?" she asked.

"No, I have one." I reached down and retrieved it from my left shoe.

"You put a cuff key in your shoe?" she asked, looking puzzled. "Why?"

"Why not? You never know when you might need one," I said, cracking a little smile.

I heard the back door again and footsteps coming towards the front of the house. It sounded like just one set, but softer than Jack's. Jayson walked in and nodded at me, then sat down on the couch.

"Sorry I'm late for the show. What did I miss?" he asked.

"Jack's blow out. JT sent him out," Sam explained as Jayson shook his head.

"Three-six, we do this little exercise to teach you what not to do, but in a controlled environment. You could have been killed today. Do you realize that?" Jayson waited for my response, but I didn't answer.

JT's turn. He seemed physically disturbed with me. "Why would you get into a car with a target and not tell anybody? You had no idea who she was, where you were going and you didn't report."

I didn't answer.

"Why not?" JT yelled. "Answer me! This is not a joke, Junior!"

"I should have called you, I know," I replied.

"Why didn't you?" JT continued, treating me like a thirteen-year-old who just got caught drinking for the first time.

"I thought I was going to dinner," I answered, but JT didn't like my response.

"You had no idea?" JT paused. "She's a target, three-six!" His voice grew louder.

"I didn't think she was a real target," I tried to explain, but JT cut me off.

"What do you mean you didn't think she was a real target? What did you think then?" The veins in JT's neck were becoming more and more visible.

"I thought she was a random girl at a coffee shop named Lupe that you wanted me to practice on, just like all the other assignments," I continued.

"You didn't pick up on anything she did that would tell you otherwise?" JT asked.

I paused. "No, sorry I didn't." JT, sounding frustrated, told Sam, "Get him out of my sight."

"Sam," Jayson interrupted, "I'll take him back. Go ahead and go home."

"Sir, I don't mind, I can do it," Sam replied, still seeming concerned.

"No, I got it, thanks."

Sam complied with Jayson's request and Jayson and I left. I figured Jayson must out-rank Sam because she always called him "sir" and did what he told her, displaying the utmost respect.

"Let's go, Steven. I guess we owe you dinner. Where do you want to eat?" Jayson asked.

"You don't owe me dinner, but whoever Lupe is sure does," I said, cracking a smile. Mexican – is there a good Mexican place around here?"

We got in the car and drove to a local hole-in-the-wall Mexican place on the east-side of the city.

"Jayson, do they let white people in here?" I asked as we pulled up.

Jayson ignored my comment as he exited the car shaking his head.

It was a bright yellow building with steel bars on the door and a small window displaying a proud letter "B" for a grade in the window. Not a place I would have picked, but they had great chips and salsa. We sat near the back in a corner booth. The seat was torn, with a large slash down the middle, and cold to the touch. I sat with my back to the door but I had scanned the place as we were walking in.

"Do you drink beer?" Jayson asked.

"Sure."

"Good. I don't trust anyone that doesn't drink beer. What do you want?" Jayson stared at me with his steel blue eyes.

"Are we not on duty right now? Can we do that?" I asked, showing my ignorance.

"Steven, we're past that don't you think? You just got slapped upside your head by another officer while you were handcuffed…What do you want?"

"Corona. Corona is good," I replied quickly.

The waitress brought us two Coronas, chips and salsa. Her face was worn and wrinkled. Her eyes were weathered. Mariachi music was playing from a jukebox located at the entrance, but it wasn't too loud where we were sitting. I hadn't seen a side door or a fire exit. Except for two couples enjoying their dinner and a single man reading a newspaper, the rest of the restaurant was empty.

"Jayson, excuse me, I have to go to the restroom," I said.

The restrooms were located on the other side of the restaurant near the kitchen. As I walked down the hallway, I noted a back-exit door. Then I purposely made a wrong right turn into the kitchen. A young Hispanic kid looked at me as I walked in. He was sweating profusely as he raised his right hand, pointing for me to leave and saying something in Spanish; I saw another back-screen door in the corner of the kitchen. I left and entered the restroom. It had an overwhelming smell of urine mixed with bleach. Graffiti on the wall, looked like MS13 territory, one urinal and one stall; no windows. I washed my hands; the water had a slight rust color to it, consistent with the age of the building. I dried my hands on my pants and returned to our table.

"What do you want to eat?" Jayson asked through his thick grey beard, which concealed his lips, even when he talked.

"If they have albondigas soup, I'll have a bowl and two flour tortillas with just butter," I said.

Jayson ordered two chicken tacos with rice and beans. Over the next hour and a half, we enjoyed our meals and drank a few more Coronas than we probably should have. It was nice because we didn't talk about work, UC stuff, or anything important.

"Are you done, or can you go one more?" Jayson asked, referring to the Coronas.

"Sure, let's do it," I said, as liquid courage ran through my body.

"Mija, can you give us one more round please." His eyes twinkled like Santa Claus'. "Steven. Let me ask you something. Did you really go to the restroom earlier or were you scoping out your escape routes?" he asked.

I started to laugh. "I was scoping it out, of course."

"What about the people in here? Do you have a handle on that too?"

I paused, took a drink of beer. "Sure, I do. You trained me."

"Exactly. Do you expect me to believe that bullshit you were selling to JT and Jack earlier about Lupe?" He turned, set down his beer and stared directly into my eyes. I looked away quickly, my body involuntarily shifting in the booth.

"Not sure what you mean," I said, as I regained my composure and locked eyes with him again.

"What I mean is I think you are full of shit. I think you knew Lupe was a plant the whole time, because to be honest, she's not that good." There was silence as we continued to lock eyes. "You're too good not to have picked up on something. The only thing I can't figure out is why you're telling JT and Jack that you didn't know anything. What's up?" Jayson took a drink of his Corona, then leaned back against the cushion, releasing a puff of air from the cushion's crack as he awaited my response.

"Jayson, it's just easier with them. They think they know me and they never have anything good to say, so I didn't want to go through it with them. I got their little exercise. It was good. I learned. That's it," I said truthfully.

Jayson leaned forward again, "Bullshit. Here's my problem. I knew you figured it out with Lupe and you did it anyway. That's what scares me. The bigger problem I have is, why would an undercover go into a house that he knows is a set up?" Jayson seemed upset, yet intrigued.

"Yeah, I knew… I was a little upset with myself because I didn't know until I got into the car. After that I knew the whole time," I explained.

"Even worse, kid!" Jayson's voice rose as he set down his beer. "You and I both know that you knew, so why would you walk into the house? It's not a game with a win or lose result. We're in the intelligence-gathering business, Steven. If we do our job right, no one knows that we're even there, where the information came from, and the Department will never even publicly acknowledge your existence. Our 'win', to use your terms, is stealth, and the public will never know what we did."

I didn't answer him as I began to process what he was saying. There was a significant pause. Then I squared and faced him. "I don't have an ego, Jayson."

"So why did you go in the house?" Jayson replied quickly.

"I knew it wasn't for real, so I wanted to see what they had in store for me. I figured I could handle it. I didn't think I was going to get choked out and handcuffed though. Who the fuck does that? Is that even legal? Can they do that shit?" The Coronas began to take over my vocabulary.

"Steven, I get that reasoning, but the play was don't go in the house. I think your ego led you in that house because you thought you could handle it and that wasn't the case now was it? Real life, you'd be torched, dead," Jayson said in a disappointed tone.

"I know, Jayson. If it was real life, I wouldn't have gone in the house. I promise." As we finished our fourth beers, I was feeling the effects of the alcohol.

"Steven, do you have an inner voice?" Jayson asked, seeming to accept my answer and underlying apology.

"A what?" I started to laugh.

"Inner voice. I believe all people have an inner voice, just some people refuse to hear it." He started to laugh too as he rubbed the lime around the rim of a fresh Corona. "For example, I'll be walking down a sidewalk and my inner voice will sometimes tell me go to the right of the tree instead of left, but there is no logical reason why I couldn't go left."

I looked at Jayson as if he was crazy, trying to process what he was saying.

Jayson continued, "Do you hear your inner voice, first of all, and second, do you listen and go right? Or another example, playing blackjack in Vegas, has your inner voice ever told you to hit or maybe stay, when the odds or book tells you not to?"

"Are you talking about intuition?" I asked.

"No, not at all. Intuition is a feeling. This is stronger; it is literally a voice in your head or maybe a vivid dream that comes true," Jayson explained adamantly.

"Are you serious? You believe in that stuff?" I asked, thinking he might be bullshitting me.

"It's not a matter of believing, Steven. It's true. I know that it's just a matter of training yourself to listen to your voice. You see, I believe that the human mind is fascinating and that we have yet to even tap into our mind's potential. I have trained myself and a few others who were willing to try to tap into what I believe is an area of the mind that might save your butt someday."

"How so?"

"Start off slow and begin to hear your inner voice. Even if it's a simple thing like you're driving in the number one lane on the freeway and your voice tells you that you should cross over to the slow lane. Listen to it and do it. Start working on it and we'll talk about it more next month." Jayson looked at his watch and took a drink.

"Sure, why not. I trust you," I said. "I'll give it a shot."

Jayson began to laugh as he took another swig of his Corona. He placed the bottle down and looked me in the eye, sitting up straight.

"Steven, don't trust me. Don't trust anyone as an undercover officer but yourself, do you understand? Don't trust your mom, girlfriend, Scooter, Gary, JT, your handlers, no one. Take it from me."

"Why, what happened to you, Jayson?" I asked, sensing something serious had happened to him.

"Just trust what I'm saying on this." Jayson raised his Corona bottle. "To Tuesday, test day. Great job, Steven."

I started to laugh as I drank the last of my beer. "Hey, Sam said Fridays were test days, not Tuesdays," I exclaimed as we both got up to leave.

"Every day as an undercover is a test day, Steven. Don't forget that." Jayson put his arm around me as we left.

Liz

March 15, 1995 – the following day I was scheduled to leave Los Angeles for Maryland to research and write my new identity's background. It was time to face Liz and tell her about my assignment and I was fearful that our relationship would be over.

It was unusually cold that night. I remember pulling into her driveway and she must have seen my truck's lights when I pulled in because she was already out the door headed down the walkway. Her hair was pulled back, accenting the diamond earrings we'd bought her in Vegas. A scarf wrapped twice around her neck, black mini-skirt over her black leggings to keep her legs warm, finished off with her favorite black boots. Our eyes locked and her smile consumed her face as she followed it with a hug and kiss. The familiar smell of Chanel took over the air. I grabbed her hand as we walked towards my truck.

"Oh, babe, your hands are so sweaty. What's wrong? Are you okay?" Liz asked.

"No, I'm okay. How was your day?" I asked her as I opened my truck door. Her skirt rose up as she climbed aboard, exposing the leggings hugging her inner thighs.

"My day was shitty, but nothing that you and Don Jose margarita can't fix," she said.

She climbed into my truck as her head shook from side to side. I didn't crack my usual joke or respond at all. A rare silence unfolded between us as Liz began to process my non-response. I was overcome with doubt about my decision and wished I'd handled the process better, but it was too late now. I hadn't really told her much, nor had I been completely honest with her, only because I had never really been sure this assignment was real or that I was actually going to get selected and go through with it. I'd known I was about ready to throw away the best relationship I'd ever had – she was a great woman – and all for the unknown.

"Liz, I need to talk to you about an opportunity that I was chosen for at work that will affect our relationship." My voice cracked slightly.

"What do you mean?" she responded as we pulled into the parking lot of Don Jose's.

"Let's go get some dinner and I'll tell you." I put the car in park.

"Drew MacGregor, you tell me right now." Her speech quickened.

"I will over dinner, I promise." I got out of the truck to grab her door for her, but uncharacteristically she was already outside waiting for me; we held hands and walked inside to our favorite table. Michelle was working, so she automatically brought our chips, salsa, and margaritas just the way we liked them.

"Babe, I was offered a job to work the Anti-Terrorist Division out of Headquarters. I'm told that only a handful of officers have ever been chosen to work this assignment and it will be a huge benefit to my career."

"Well that's great!" she said as her smile widened and her shoulders relaxed. "But how does that affect us? Is it dangerous or something? It sounds exciting," she continued.

"Yes, it can be dangerous I'm told, but so is police work in general. The problem is that it's an undercover assignment and I have to give them a three-year commitment from the time I'm trained…"

"Undercover? Like the movies."

"Yes, I guess it's like the movies, but this is for real."

"I don't understand?" She leaned back into the lime green chair and folded her arms.

"Basically, I assume another person's identity and my job would be to try and bust terrorists."

"You're not serious," she said, cracking a smile, hoping to get a positive reaction.

"I am serious, babe. I swear, I'm not joking."

"But you work for the police department, right? Police departments don't bust terrorists or have undercover officers like the movies… do they?" She sat up straighter.

"I didn't think they did either but they do. You can't tell anyone what I'm telling you or I can get in big trouble," I said.

"I don't understand. This all sounds crazy to me." Her voice was getting louder.

"I know. It is crazy, babe." I reached my hand across the distressed wooden table for her hand, but she just looked at it as she processed what I was telling her.

"So, are you saying that you will be moving to the *city* for three years?" Her eyes widened as she continued to try and wrap her head around something that I had had five months to process.

"I don't know where I will be yet, but even if I did, or when I do know, I can't tell you," I tried to explain.

"What do you mean you can't tell me? We love each other and we're going to get married!" Liz's voice began to crack and her eyes began to well up. The couple sitting next to us turned and looked at her.

"I can't tell you where I will be or what I will be doing. You can't even have my phone number and I can't call you on a regular basis, but you would be able to write me."

"So, if you take this job, I can't see you or call you for three years? Is that what you're saying?" Her eyes took a bead on mine and her nose flared just slightly.

"No, no, not exactly. I can call you sometimes, but I don't know when or how often. We can see each other, I'm told, but I don't know how often yet. Maybe, once every three to four months," I tried to explain.

"Seriously? I don't know that I can do that, Mac. That would be hard, don't you think? Why would you do that? Why would you do that to us!" Liz was yelling now.

"Well, the money is good and they tell me it will set my career up. I think it would be good for us when I'm done."

"Yeah, but it's three fucking years, Mac. That's like a prison sentence… we won't make it." She unfolded her arms.

"Yes, we can, babe, I think we can do it," I said, again reaching for her hand.

"When do you have to let them know your decision?" she asked.

I paused.

"Mac, when do you have to let them know?" she asked again, this time with more urgency.

151

I looked away.

"You told them yes already didn't you!" Her voice grew loud again.

"Yes, I did," I replied quietly, knowing that I was about to get it.

"Are you serious?! You told them yes without even talking to me about it? Seriously, Mac! You joke about us getting married and we say that we love each other and then you make this decision without ever talking to me?" Liz's eyes began to fill with tears.

"Liz, I do love you," I said, hoping that catch-all phrase would get me somewhere.

"Stop! Don't say that to me anymore. You lost that right. People that love each other don't keep secrets like this!" She was officially pissed now.

"Liz, what are you talking about?"

She tried to hold back her tears. "You know, Mac, I think this whole thing is bullshit. Nobody does this. If you want to break up with me, be a man and just do it. Don't come up with this bullshit story. Who is she? Is there another girl?"

"No Liz…"

She cut me off, "Stop! Take me home!" Her hands began to wave side-to-side as her Latina spirit awakened and transitioned her from the emotional upset stage to just plain pissed off. She began to rattle off words in Spanish at high speed as she stood up.

"Liz... Let's..." I tried to speak.

She cut me off again. "I said stop!" Her voice was loud enough for people to look over at us again. "I said take me home and if you won't I'll call my sister." She walked outside. I left forty dollars on the table and walked outside after her. She was crying hysterically, but more pissed than hurt. I tried to comfort her, but she pushed me away, followed by a nice right cross to my chest, and continued to walk towards my truck.

Training Module No. 5

Two days later, I was on a plane from the city to Virginia with a mission to research and write the background story for Steven Mathew's life. My tasks included creating Steven's life, documenting it, photographing it, and most important of all, memorizing it. Over the next two weeks, I traveled to schools, libraries, towns, bars, churches, farms, restaurants, gas stations, sporting events, movie theaters, grocery stores, barber shops, malls, car dealerships, town halls, rivers and lakes. As I explored and traveled through the cities and towns, I began to write my new life. I began to live Steven's life as I developed it. Where he went to school; where his best friends lived; relatives lived; where he hung out; where he worked; everything I could think of that people know about themselves without even thinking about it. I spent every minute, hour, days, weeks… in the library, looking through old news events from my new home town: fires, explosions, etc. I talked to every local or old timer who would give me the time, and I wrote everything down in a green hardback notebook.

One of my key objectives on my travels was to obtain an out-of-state driver's license and I chose the Virginia Department of Motor Vehicles. As I walked into the DMV, my stomach was in knots and my hands began to sweat. It was a small DMV, unlike the dreaded California lines I was accustomed to. A small counter top with what appeared to be two windows for assistance. An eight-point deer head mounted to the wall appeared to be their security guard as he overlooked the room. A brown-aired, middle-aged woman sitting on a high-back office chair, about counter height, made eye contact with me as I walked in the door.

"Hi there, young man." She had a natural friendly smile and spoke with a high-pitched voice followed by an eastern drawl.

"Good morning, ma'am, I just got out of the military and I need to get my driver's license. Can you help me with that?" I asked.

"Well thank you for your service young man. Hun, do you have the paperwork already?"

"Yes, ma'am, I believe so. Here you are." I handed her the application form which I had previously printed out.

"Thank you, sir." She paused as she reviewed the application. "You're twenty-five years of age and you haven't gotten your driver's license yet?" Disappointment came across in her tone.

"No, ma'am. The military has kept me pretty busy over the years," I answered, just as I was trained.

"I'll get you fixed up and thank you again for serving our country." Her voice changed again, reassuring now.

"Thank you so much! What's your name?" I asked, trying to make a connection.

"Nancy," she replied.

"Well, Nancy, it's nice to meet you and thank you again for helping me. It's been a rough move out here from California, but I love it here," I continued, trying to build a rapport.

"Steven, do you have your proof of residence and ID with you?" she asked.

"Sure, here you are," I said, handing her a copy of an electric bill that I had taken from an unknown mail box. I'd used white-out over the name, address and account number, changing them to mine before photocopying it at a local store.

"Perfect, thank you, and your original birth certificate?" Nancy inquired.

"No ma'am, I don't have that. All of my stuff is still in California, but I called and they told me that two forms of ID would work instead."

"Sure, that'll work." Nancy smiled.

"Great, here you are." I handed her a fake military photo identification that I'd made back in Los Angeles by pasting my academy photograph onto a fake military template then laminating it. I also handed her a library card with my photo that I had obtained the day before at the local library.

"Great. Thank you, Steven," Nancy answered, then turned and walked away out of my sight, holding my two fake identification cards along with my application. I began to panic slightly. "She knows. I'm done," ran through my brain. My hands began to sweat even more profusely. Every part of me felt like I was in trouble and I wanted to flee. It was the classic flight or fight syndrome and I recognized it. *Okay, Drew, remember your training and don't panic. What are you going to say if she questions you?* I thought to myself as I saw Nancy turn the corner and head back towards me.

"Steven, here is your paperwork and your identifications back. Please have a seat over there and someone will be out to administer the driving test."

"Yes, ma'am," I answered, but my legs wouldn't move yet as I turned to walk back to the seating area. A sense of accomplishment quickly turned to panic again. *Driving test? Drew, you forgot about the driving test.* I started to laugh inside.

A few minutes went by, then, "Steven, they will meet you outside for your driving test," Nancy called out.

"Yes, ma'am," I answered and walked outside.

I walked out to the car; as I climbed into the driver's seat, I grabbed a few papers with my real name on them and threw them under the seat. For the next twenty minutes, I drove around Virginia's streets as the instructor evaluated me on my driving skill and knowledge much like when I was sixteen.

"Congratulations, Steven, you got a ninety-six. Take this back in to Nancy and she will help you," the instructor said as we came to a stop.

"Yes, ma'am. Thank you."

I walked back inside the DMV like a peacock, feathers on full display, my chest high as I handed my paperwork back to Nancy at the counter.

After a few minutes, Nancy called out "Steven?" and motioned with her hand for me to step up to the counter again.

"Yes, ma'am," I responded.

"I'm sorry, but we can't give you a driver's license today," she said with a frown.

"Why not?" I asked.

"Well, your name came up with a *hit* on it so I can't issue your license until they clear it."

"A hit? What does that mean?" I was pissed inside because I knew exactly what it meant. How could JT have given me a name with a hit on it? What a dumb ass, I thought. Was he still testing me?

"A *hit* means that there is something in your background associated with your name where I am not allowed to give you a license until it is cleared. It generally is someone with the same name. Don't worry, I'm sure you will be fine," Nancy said in a reassuring voice.

"Okay, how long does that take, because I need it now just to get my own apartment and to live," I said, attempting to get her to bend the rules.

"I'm sorry, I understand, but it will probably take two weeks or so," Nancy explained.

"Shoot, I'll be back in California getting my stuff by then and I need a license to drive back here. Can you mail it to California or do I have to come pick it up?"

"No, sir, I can mail it to California for you. No problem, just give me an address," she assured me.

Two weeks later, I arrived back in California with a new life in my hands. I had documents, photos, and mountains of information from Virginia; now I just had to commit it to memory. Over the next week, JT and his crew tested me over and over on my background, trying to plug the holes in it.

The next day JT told me to call David at 0900 hours and he would advise me where to report. After my success in Virginia, my energy and morale were high. I called David and he told me to meet him in the parking lot of a Denny's located out in the Valley. When I arrived, I saw David's car backed into the first parking stall; so typical of a cop. He motioned me to get into the car.

"Hey David, what's shakin'?" I asked as I climbed into his car.

"What's up, Drew? Just hang out for a minute."

We were just sitting in his car and I could sense something was up. An awkward silence filled the car.

"Hey David, I'll be right back. I'm going to hit the *head*." I opened the car door and began to leave.

"No! You can't go. Get back into the car we have to go," David exclaimed.

"David, I really have to go, do we have time?" I asked.

"No, I said just get in the car!" David reiterated as I looked at him with a perplexed look, trying to gauge whether or not he was joking or being serious.

"Okay, but can you tell me what's going on?" I asked.

"Yeah, your number came up for drug testing. I'm waiting to see where I'm supposed to take you so you can pee in a cup," David told me straight up.

"You guys think I'm on drugs? Seriously? What the fuck? That's messed up. *Trust*, my ass?" I opened the car door and stepped outside.

"Drew, I'm not joking, and if you leave you will be out of the program. All of that work for nothing. Do you have something to hide?" David asked.

"This isn't about hiding anything. This is all a game to you guys. It's one way. You guys never tell me shit and expect me to go along with everything you say like your little puppet. *Do you have the right and need to know shit* is all I ever hear. You guys either start treating me as a partner in this game or you can count me out," I yelled.

"Okay, David, it's clear, bring him in," a deep voice blurted across a hidden radio in the car.

David told me he was going to take me to a Department of Water and Power facility where two detectives would meet me to drug test me. There wouldn't be any other employees there and the detectives wouldn't ask me my name or assignment. "Just go in there, pee in the cup, and leave," he said. "We'll be outside guarding the door and making sure no one comes in."

I went into the first floor where I found two detectives dressed in suits. Typical cop appearance: short hair, stern grouchy looks on their faces, with their heads on a swivel.

"Hey boys. Where do you want me to go?"

My question and small talk were met with silence as they directed me to a bathroom on the second floor.

"You guys are from the Police Department?" I asked.

The guy with the salt and pepper hair turned back and looked bothered by my question as he opened the door for me. An awkward situation for both of us as he handed me a bag with two cups inside, still not saying a word.

"Any special directions on this?" I asked again, trying to get a response.

He still wasn't responding to my version of humor. "Sir, please fill. I need both of them filled up to the line, if you can." He'd finally spoken – *goal accomplished, I guess*, my inner voice blurted out in my head.

"Will do," I said with a smirk on my face.

I peed into both cups and handed him the warm containers and they left without saying a word. It was pretty comical, looking back on it. What must a police officer have done to end his career carrying around warm pee? To this day, I still don't know the answer.

My formal training was complete, and now I was assigned to my handlers full time.

"Steven, it's official. You no longer have to report to those *jack wagons* over at the training unit. You're done with them and you only have to go back there for quarterly training or any admin duties you might need," Albert said with disgust; he obviously disliked them.

"Oh wow, so I won't see them anymore until my quarterly training?" This surprised me.

"No, they'll help you move out of your place but that's it. That will be your last contact with them until your quarterlies come around. You're all mine and Claire's now." Albert's chest swelled as he spoke.

"Okay, so now what?" I asked, curious.

"You need to go find a place to live out in the valley somewhere. Get a one bedroom, not a two bedroom or a studio. Your price range should be around five hundred a month. When you find a place to stay, submit the address to me and I'll get it approved."

Albert turned and left.

Time to Fly

"Never explain – your friends do not need it and your enemies will not believe you anyhow."

Elbert Hubbard

Liz

My move date was set and Liz and I weren't talking too much. Rightly
so; she was very upset that I hadn't told her, or to use her words, *shared*
my new job offer with her from the beginning. She doubted that I loved
her.

"Hi, it's me. Can I see you tonight? I think we need to have some
closure on this one way or another don't you?" I pleaded.

"I agree, but I'm still sick to my stomach," she said.

"Would it be okay if I came over and we just went for a walk?" I
pleaded.

I drove over to Liz's house. I was doubtful our relationship could
survive my undercover assignment and thought it would most likely end
it but I wanted to try to keep it intact if I could. I pulled up to her sister's
house and Liz opened the door. A ponytail protruding out of the back of
a blue Dodgers baseball cap, no makeup, gray sweat pants, with a blue
hoodie and white Vans tennis shoes. Her eyes were puffy, face
discolored, and her smile was absent. My heart broke to see her like that
and I began to feel guilty again, but I said nothing. We hugged, and I felt
her heart beat on my chest. We began to walk.

"Liz, I'm…"

She stopped me mid-sentence, grabbed my hand and looked up at me. "Can I go first?" she pleaded.

"Sure," I said.

"Drew, I love you with all my heart and I know that you are the man I want to marry. I can't live without you and I don't want to live without you. I will wait for you. I love you. We can do this, together." Her eyes welled up and she hugged me tightly.

Emotions rushed through my body. As we sat down on some grass by a local school, my inner voice began to rapidly scroll thoughts across my brain, like a NY stock exchange ticker:

You should ask her to marry you…

There's no way this is going to work…

How is this going to work, you should just end it…

"Mac, how are we going to do this?" she asked. "I mean, can I call you? Can I see you? How will I know if you're okay?" She was rambling and I could feel her hands beginning to sweat.

"Babe, to be honest I'm not sure exactly how it will work. What I do know is that you won't be able to call me directly. I will be assigned to what's called *handlers*. I have two of them; Albert and Claire are their names. They will be your pipeline to me. If you need to get hold of me, you will call them and they will have me call you when it's safe. They also say we can see each other three or four times a year for a couple of days each," I said with growing excitement.

"Really? How would that work?" Liz answered cautiously, but with excitement of her own.

"Well, again, I'm not exactly sure, but from what they tell me, they will make arrangements for us to get away somewhere safe for a couple of days three times a year. They say they'll take care of everything. Crazy, right?"

"Mac, are you sure? This sounds too crazy and not real to me. Are you sure about all of this?" Liz's excitement was already turning to doubt.

"Babe, to be honest I'm not sure of anything right now, but I have to trust them and you have to trust me. I need you and want you by my side through this, but I don't want to ask you to stay if you don't want to. It's going to be very hard I'm sure, especially since I can't talk to you about what I'm doing. You need to decide for yourself, but I'm in. I love you." I looked into her eyes to read her response.

"I love you too and I'm for sure going to wait for you. You are my *man* and no one else's! I'm just scared and all of my friends keep telling me this isn't real. They say that you're lying to me and that you probably have another girl somewhere or even another secret family like you see on Jerry Springer." She started to laugh, but I could tell she still wanted some reassurance from me.

I chuckled too. "Yes, it's real, babe, and no, I don't have a secret family somewhere. It's not the Jerry Springer Show, but now that you say that, I can see their point. Come on, let's get out of here." I grabbed her hand and stood up. "Margaritas?" I asked.

"Absolutely!" Liz answered, and as her beautiful smile appeared on her face, she jumped into my arms and wrapped her legs around my waist. "You have to carry me all the way back to my sister's house now, Mr. MacGregor," she demanded.

"Piece of cake, lady. You are five-foot-nothing and only weigh a buck soaking wet! I got this."

I started the walk back to her sister's house as Liz held on tight, squeezing her legs around my waist, and began kissing my neck.

"Hey! You can't do that. That's cheating!" I exclaimed, but my protest fell on deaf ears.

"Don't be a sore loser! You can't stand to lose, can you, Mr. MacGregor, but you are going down this time." She chuckled and looked at me with a devilish grin. Next thing I knew, she'd launched a full-frontal attack, kissing me, tickling me, climbing higher up on my torso and putting her breasts in my face, shaking them back and forth.

"Cheater, foul… foul! That's against the rules. You can't do that," I continued to protest as I started to lose my grip. She didn't let up and finally I had to let go. Liz fell out of my arms. Her feet hit the ground and she burst into an immediate victory dance, or at least that was what she called it.

"Boom! I just took down the almighty Mr. MacGregor. Oh yeah baby! Oh yeah baby!" Pointing at me with both hands, prancing around, and jumping up and down, spinning around free as can be, just like the old days. She broke into a leaning squat *raising the roof* with both hands up in the air. "Whoop, whoop, that's right baby!" she continued, as I fell deeper in love with her at that very moment.

I laughed, "It's not the Super Bowl, you big dork."

She ignored my feeble attempt to downplay her victory and continued gloating for the rest of the night.

Moving Day

My dad arrived from Arizona to say goodbye and to take some of my personal belongings back to Arizona for storage. When he arrived, we loaded up his truck with the personal stuff that wouldn't be making the journey with me.

"Thanks for taking my stuff, dad. Do you guys have time to stay for dinner with Liz and me?" I asked.

"No, son, we have to get back on the road." He reached out to give me a hug.

"Are you sure? I don't know when I'll be able to see you again," I asked one last time because I didn't want him to go so soon.

"Next time, son. We have to get on the road. It's a long drive," he insisted.

I gave him one last hug, granting his wish to leave and trying not to take it personally. I saw him reach into his front pocket and pull out a shiny object.

"Here, bud. I want to give you this, it kept me safe in Korea and it will bring you luck." A 1918 silver dollar that he'd carried around with him since the war. I remembered seeing it in his pocket a few times growing up, yet it had never struck me to ask him why. He handed me the silver dollar and quickly turned to get into his truck. I could tell he was choked up, however; MacGregors aren't very good at showing their sentimental side. "MacGregors don't cry, son," I'd heard from my pops numerous times growing up.

Before I knew it, he was in his truck and they were driving off; surreal to me as I walked back into the house holding the coin in my hand. Looking back, all the thoughts that I think most kids ponder as they enter adulthood and even beyond rushed through my head at once. Was my dad disappointed because I'd chosen law enforcement instead of medicine? What did he really think? I wished he would just tell me. I guessed I was hoping for him to say, "Son, I'm proud of you and everything will be all right." I wanted his reassurance like all kids do from their parents. I was scared and doubting my decision. I never got that from my dad that day in words; his approval came instead in the symbolism of the silver dollar.

I spent the remainder of the morning pacing around the house soaking up memories. I felt strange... part of me felt as if I was going on a long vacation and another part felt as if I might not be coming back at all. A calming silence fell over the air that morning and I didn't know why. The phone didn't ring. I couldn't hear kids walking to the nearby school, and the elderly people that lived on our block weren't out spying from their porches.

I took the dogs out front and sat on the lawn with them. Justice, my German Shepherd, who I'd rescued from the dog pound the previous Valentine's Day, walked curiously around the yard snooping around for anything. Kalua, Gary's Rot, followed her, nipping at her tail, wanting to play, but Justice wasn't having any of it.

Suddenly, I looked up and saw two vehicles pulling up in front of my house. Both vehicles were American made; four doors, with blacked-out windows and current December registration tags. David, Jack, Sam, and JT piled out of the cars. I greeted them, but I was unusually quiet that morning. I backed the U-Haul trailer into my driveway as JT's crew began to inspect the belongings I'd gathered together to be loaded onto it. They were looking for anything I'd missed that might identify me as Drew MacGregor. After my belongings had been inspected, they were loaded onto the trailer.

"Is that everything, Steven?" David asked.

"Yeah I think so. I'm ready," I said with a tentative voice.

I walked over and gave my dogs a last hug and kiss and jumped into the driver's seat of the U-Haul. The trailer made a loud clunking noise as I backed out of the driveway. Pulling away slowly, gazing in the enormous side view mirrors of the U-Haul, Drew's life slowly disappeared from my view.

I arrived at Steven Mathew's apartment approximately an hour and a half later. It was located in a lower-class neighborhood in a suburb of the Valley. My apartment house was orange and had bars on the windows and security gates surrounding it. The grass was dying out front and there were several bare patches of dirt. When we arrived, a sprinkler head was spouting water straight up into the air and the water ran down the sidewalk and into the street. The living conditions were bearable, but definitely would take some getting used to on my part.

My apartment, a one bedroom on the upstairs level, was a corner unit, approximately six-hundred-square-feet in all. It consisted of three rooms total: the main, living room, separated by a lime-green Formica counter-top on the right side where a small kitchen resided and straight ahead, through a small hallway, was my new master bedroom equipped with a small closet and a single bathroom containing the same lime-green Formica. The carpet was dark brown and the walls were a beige color. The apartment had a fresh paint smell that masked an unidentifiable musty odor.

I unloaded and arranged all my old stuff in my new apartment. My old bed, college-style with just box springs and no frame, was shoved against the corner in the bedroom. My comforter was black and I had brought my two favorite pillows, one large one and a second medium sized. My nightstands consisted of two blue milk crates draped with black towels to cover the dirt and rust on the frames and lastly, the couch my aunt had given me when I'd gone away to college was placed in the living room. It was old, tearing on the left arm, and contained a distinct smell I couldn't describe, but it wasn't pungent. The couch was the only real symbol I'd taken with me that provided me with some weird sense of security or at least familiarity from my previous life. JT's crew placed the remainder of my belongings in the middle of the two-room apartment and JT said, "Let's go eat."

"Sure, I'm hungry," I replied.

We climbed into the plain wrap police cars and drove to a local In-N-Out Burger around the corner from my new apartment. I ordered my usual – number one, no onions, add pickles, with a large Coke – which I never finished. Once I'd sat down to eat, I began to realize that this was the big day. I was scared and still unsure of what to expect from the whole program. I ate my lunch and held my head high, not letting anyone from JT's crew know what emotions were running through my head.

After lunch, JT asked to see me at the back of his car. When we got there, he said, "Before we get out of here, I need your badge and gun, Junior. I'll give it back, I promise, in three years when you get out."

As I reached for my badge, my heart dropped and a slight sickness in my stomach suddenly appeared. That statement seemed more like a prison sentence. Three years! Wow... it seemed like forever to me right then.

I had worked so hard for this badge and now I had to give it up. I guessed I'd known this moment was coming and I'd truly believed it wouldn't be that big of a deal for me. I was wrong: that badge had come to mean much more than just the number inscribed on the front of it, 11063. The old timers had always joked that my badge number seemed more like a zip code than a badge number, it was so long. However, the badge was mine; it represented my pride, sweat, determination, achievement, and most of all, my integrity. From the moment that badge had been pinned on my chest, I'd coveted and accepted the

176

responsibilities that accompanied it. It had been one of the proudest moments of my life at that time. I often shined my badge for up to an hour, making sure every crevice was polished. I felt the badge represented who you were, and most of all, who you could be. I was proud to wear the badge of a Los Angeles Police Officer.

I reached into my back-right pocket and pulled out a black leather wallet. I opened the wallet up and pulled back the leather flap covering my badge. As I pulled away the leather flap the badge shone, reading, POLICE OFFICER across the top with a picture of City Hall.

JT said, "What are you doing, Junior? Let's go, I have to leave."

"Just taking a last look," I said.

JT shook his head in disbelief or disgust, I wasn't quite sure which.

I took everything out of my wallet and placed it in a black briefcase. MacGregor's CDL, my wallet, some miscellaneous documents and a picture of each of my friends and family. Sad, but that briefcase contained Drew MacGregor's life in a nutshell. Next, I pulled out my 9mm Smith &Wesson that I had concealed in my front waistband. I flipped the decocker down, conducted a chamber check, put the decocker back up, then down again as I'd been trained. Next I released the magazine and placed it in the briefcase, then locked the slide to the rear of the weapon, catching the ejecting hollow-point 9mm round with my left hand as it exited the chamber. I placed the extra 9mm round in the briefcase next to the magazine, released the slide and conducted one last chamber check. I paused for a second, then placed the cleared weapon in the briefcase.

Having gone through two police academies and received countless hours of training on what happened to police officers who gave up their weapons, I couldn't help but wonder if my fate would fall into the same category or statistic. I had just given up my weapon and police identification; what were my chances of surviving now? I knew that I'd said I would give up my badge and gun back in the interviews, but now I realized that it was easier said than done. I felt naked without a gun... I had just been stripped of my last physical tool as a police officer.

JT closed the briefcase and placed it on the front seat of his car. "Okay, Junior," he said, "I think we're done here. Your first item of business is to find a job somewhere local. Keep me updated on your progress. You good?"

Not waiting for my response, he glanced at his watch and climbed into his car and left. Recognizing what time it was, I realized they were all at the End of Watch – time for them to go home.

My new ride in my new life was an old pickup truck that had been stripped. It was black and contained none of the extra amenities I was accustomed to. It didn't have air conditioning, a radio, a nice paint job, or rims, and it ran like shit. As I started to drive back to the apartment, I knew this was going to be harder than I'd expected. I didn't know if I could even live like this for six months, let alone live like this *and* do the undercover job. I had been raised with a great deal of self-pride and respect which spilled over into my personal life and was going to be difficult to suppress. I was used to having nice things and being able to go out and get whatever I wanted, within reason, of course.

I arrived back at my new apartment, walked through the security gates and up the stairs to apartment No. 284, my new home. I unlocked all the locks and opened the door and sat in the middle of my apartment next to the remainder of my belongings, and my emotions began to flow. I felt so alone, as if I had moved to another planet. I knew that I had only moved approximately a hundred miles away, but the world as I knew it was forever gone, or at least it felt that way. I wanted to call my mom just to hear her voice, but I refrained from it. Having been in martial arts for years, I relied upon the discipline that had been instilled in me and I didn't call.

My first night in the apartment was one of the longest nights of my life; it seemed as if it took forever for the light to shine through my window. I lay in my bed as my mind raced and my wheels turned minute after minute, then hour after hour. I heard every sound, the sirens, cars passing, neighbors yelling and screaming at each other, and babies crying.

"I fucked up, this is not right," I said to myself.

It was just a feeling I had. It came with no explanation or justification, but I couldn't get it out of my head. *What do I do now? Do I quit? Do I run back to my mommy?* Tears began to run down my face.

"Suck it up. You are a MacGregor and MacGregors don't cry!" I heard my dad's voice say in my head.

The next few days I was tasked with getting my electric, water, phone, and cable turned on. These tasks took me a few days to complete and cost several hundred dollars. Steven Mathews didn't have any financial history, therefore I was required to leave huge amounts of cash deposits to get my utilities turned on.

Most of my major objectives were completed now except for one last one… finding a job. It was a direct measure of how a bird could use and apply his undercover skills, his determination, and his ability to accomplish a task on his own without any guidance or assistance.

JT's crew had advised me to go get a couple of applications working in construction or as a maintenance worker, but I wasn't crazy about those ideas. They just seemed like back-breaking jobs to me that didn't pay any money…

"JT. It's Steven. I'm struggling with this job thing and I just want to clarify a few things. My employment has to be in construction or as a maintenance worker for three years? What for?"

JT responded, "Junior, we have been doing this for years, have you ever worked undercover before?"

I didn't answer him.

JT continued, "Listen to me, I know what I'm talking about. Just do it and don't question me, fuck! I thought we were past this." He hung up.

The next day, I got the local paper and circled different labor jobs, sticking with JT's plan, but I couldn't find anything, and besides, they were all minimum wage. That night I figured out that I basically needed to make ten dollars an hour just to cover my expenses and I wasn't going to settle for a job that didn't pay me at least that. After two weeks of searching I still hadn't received any job offers to my liking… I had got a job offer at the local McDonalds, but I just couldn't do it and I never told JT.

Beep, beep, beep, my pager went off: "932-1111." It was Sam's call sign, the four 1s indicating Code 1, a low priority call. I was strangely glad to see her page. I immediately left my apartment to go call her from my favorite 7 Eleven store – my favorite, since they tended to actually fix their pay phones.

"Hey Sam, what's up, how are you?" I asked.

"Hi, Steven, how is my long-lost boy toy?" Sam said with a chuckle.

"Starting right where you left off, I see, Samantha," I said with my own version of a chuckle.

"Oh, so formal now are we? You never call me Samantha," Sam prodded.

"I guess so… What's up? What can I do for you?" I asked.

"You tell me, Steven, what can you do for me?" Sam said. "Just kidding. Hey listen, JT and the boys would kill me if they knew I was calling you so keep your mouth shut, okay?"

"Of course. You can trust me," I said.

"Well, we'll find out I guess, Steven… Here's the deal. JT's full of shit on what he's telling you about your job. Go get a job at a department store. It's easy work, their background checks are marginal at best which I will cover for you, and the pay is decent with the opportunity to promote with future raises. You can ask for time off when you need it and have weekends off. Apply for an assistant manager or department head," Sam said.

"Seriously? Why wouldn't he tell me that?"

"No idea, but here's what you need to do. Just make shit up… make up the dates that you worked in retail as an associate, department head and assistant manager at different department stores on the East Coast. Whatever you want to get the job… make up everything. I will give you some East Coast phone numbers that will all forward to my phone and I'll give you glowing reviews if they call. For a price of course... It's that simple. You'll get a job if they want to hire you. Trust me, but you will owe me," she said with another chuckle.

"No problem, if it works!" I said, gladly.

"Hey Steven, I have to run. We'll talk later," Sam said.

"Hey Sam, thank you..." I hung up the phone, realizing that it was a huge move for Sam to have reached out to me; there would be major consequences for her if the boys ever found out what she'd done.

I had a job by the end of the week as a department head for a major retailer in the area.

Denny's

I never was much of a cook growing up. Sure, I could cook the basics, but cooking was never really my thing, most likely because I'm not a foody. I really only ate to survive and never really developed an appetite or an appreciation for food. I looked at food as a nuisance, because it was a necessity for survival, not really a pleasure for me.

I knew from training that it was important for me to quickly establish relationships as Steven Mathews. The more people who knew me as Steven could only help establish my background and cover in the future, especially now that I was working. I chose a local Denny's as my training ground, food supplier, and first background anchor for Steven. I'm not sure if any of you have ever eaten at a Denny's in the ghetto but it is definitely an experience. I knew this was going to be difficult for me because for the most part, I am a very private person. I don't like to strike up conversations with strangers; it just isn't my style.

"Good evening. Just one tonight?" asked the hostess. A young Hispanic girl, most likely about seventeen years old, short brown hair; slightly chunky by today's standards, with a face troubled with acne. On her gray shirt, she had a white name tag displaying the name "Lucia" in black lettering.

"Yes, thank you," I responded.

Lucia grabbed all four menus and walked away to show me to my table. She walked with a limp on her right side and her face seemed troubled, I didn't know why.

"How is your day going?" she asked with a Spanish accent. "Is this table okay?" She stopped at the third booth near the front exit.

"Yes, this is great. Thank you… Lucia," I responded.

Lucia walked away and I got to work. First, I checked out the kitchen, emergency exits, windows, and of course the restrooms. I surveyed the entire layout of Denny's and selected my favorite booth for my future visits. Booth number eleven was located in the corner of the L-shaped layout of the restaurant; it was tan in color, and seated four. The table top was etched with graffiti, but appeared to be clean. Magically positioned, this booth allowed me to sit with my back towards the front entrance, contrary to all law enforcement training, however, I could still see who was entering by way of a huge wall mirror located on the number four side directly in front of my seat.

"Hi, my name is Manny and I will be taking care of you today. Can I get you something to drink?" a tall slender man asked me.

"Sure, I'll take a Coke, two scrambled eggs, toast, and two pieces of bacon," I replied.

"Breakfast for dinner? I love breakfast too. I do the same thing sometimes. Sure, I'll bring it right out." Manny walked away and came back shortly with a Coke. "Here you are," he said. "Your order will be right up."

Over the next several days I repeated this process with several restaurants in and around my apartment, ensuring I knew each of the layouts inside and out. I also made sure that at least three employees knew my name and recognized my face.

The days and nights seemed so long during my first several months in my new place. I had some trouble sleeping; things improved after I started working, but I still didn't allow myself to have any friends. What was crazy was I was trying to distance myself from my real-life friends and family too, not calling any of them. I wanted to harden myself, almost like I would imagine a convicted criminal would do when he was first sentenced to a long prison term. I was struggling... I had no one to even talk to about what I was going through physically or emotionally, nor did I really understand it myself. Think about it... how many people do you talk to right now about your daily activities? What about if you had a bad day? In this case I had no one I could tell the truth to. Everything, and I mean everything, I talked about with any meaning was a lie.

The residents of my apartment complex were ninety-nine percent Hispanic and half of them didn't speak any English which didn't help me much. Cultural differences between my new and old worlds was palpable, differences I'd previously been naïve to. My previous world consisting of middle class, white, milk toast type neighborhoods; think of the *Desperate Housewives* stereotype neighborhood. All our neighbors knew each other and even worse, everyone else's personal business.

Here, many of the apartments had two families living in a one-bedroom apartment because they had so little discretionary income. Another crazy thing was there was a definite fear factor in the community. That was just crazy to me. I'd never felt unsafe in any neighborhood where I'd rested my head at night. The sound of sirens and the lights from the police helicopter or ghetto bird, as it was known where I now lived, shining in your window were now nightly occurrences. Much of this behavior was foreign to me and it added to the feelings of isolation and loneliness I was battling within myself.

One night on my way home from work, I made my first phone call to my mom. It had been almost three months since we had spoken. I pulled over to a K-Mart where I saw three pay phones in a line. Grabbing a pocketful of change, I figured my chances of at least one of the phones working were pretty good. The phone receiver had God knows what kind of fungus on it and smelled worse than usual. As I dialed my mother's phone number a voice called out, "Three dollars for the first three minutes."

"Three bucks, damn," I said as I put the change in the box.

My mom answered the phone, "Hello." Her voice was so soothing to me. There is nothing better than hearing your mother's voice as a deep undercover officer.

"Hey, Ma," I said.

She was so happy to hear my voice she began talking right away like I knew she would. I just sat and listened, not offering any information in return. When that voice returned, "One dollar for the next three minutes," I said, "Ma, I gotta go. I don't have any more change, but I will call you again soon, I promise."

"Drew, are you okay?" she asked.

"Yeah, Ma, I'll call ya in a couple of weeks," I said as I hung up.

She knew I was lying. My mom is one of the few people who can tell when I am upset, intuitively, like most mothers I'm sure. Mother's instinct.

A bird must maintain phone security at all times, something which was stressed to the max in my training, but it was such a pain in my ass. A bird cannot use the phone in his apartment to call anyone in Drew's life or his life as a police officer, because that would be considered a cross-over and could jeopardize my safety. There were so many times I just wanted to pick up my home phone and call my girlfriend, mom, dad, and friends. Who would know?

But I knew that the phone security was in place not only for my safety but for the person I was calling too, so I followed it religiously. It had to be crazy for my parents too… If they wanted to talk to me, my parents had to page my handlers and wait for a phone call back. My handlers would then get hold of me and tell me to call whoever had made the request.

Date Night

Several people from my cover job at the retail store were going to a club in Los Angeles where one our co-workers, Dominick, moonlighted as a bouncer. The best thing about it was that Dom could get us all in free, no cover. I had been talking to a girl named Emily a lot at the time, a friend of Maria who worked in the housewares department at our store. Emily lived in the neighborhood and would frequently come in to visit Maria and eventually me. We'd had several lunches together but had never been out on an official date. It was safe to say that we were not dating, but we enjoyed each other's company and had spent several hours on the phone together over the past few weeks.

Emily was a stunning girl, a year younger than me, five-foot-five in height and about a-hundred-and-fifteen pounds. Emily's hair was long and flowed evenly down her shoulders, resting just at the small of her back. Her eyes, round and full, were a soothing deep brown, and her body was firm, showing her youth. Her chest was full, accenting her curvaceous body with very soft, golden brown skin. Emily oozed sexuality, but didn't act like she knew it.

A perplexing situation for me in my new world. Now, I fully understood why JT had told me that Liz, my girl back home, had had to go. Crystal clear, why Sam had said I was too nice for this assignment. The situation that I was in was a no-win situation. You see, one of the most important things necessary for an undercover officer to be successful is to have a girlfriend. Think of it this way: Steven would be much safer or legitimized with a girlfriend, because she will check out, no matter what. However, there were competing forces at play because I had a real girlfriend back home, yet my own safety would greatly improve if I had another girlfriend in my life as Steven. Moral and ethical decision here? You tell me...

I hadn't spoken to Liz but twice over the last several months and what with speaking with Emily almost every night, I had started to have feelings for her... or did I? The way I looked at it – or maybe rationalized it, looking back – in my head was... Mac's girlfriend was Liz, but Steven had feelings for Emily. We were two different people living inside the same body.

As I pulled up in front of Emily's apartment to pick her up for the evening, a stunning silhouette appeared. Emily was wearing a black cocktail dress that hugged her body, stopping about mid-thigh. Two small straps lay across her chest and flowed over her shoulders, meeting in the middle of her back, leaving just enough skin exposed. As she walked from the darkness into the moonlight my heart began to race. Emily walked up to me and gave me a hug and a kiss on my cheek before she climbed into my car. As I hugged her, her smell transferred to my shirt.

There were ten of us together, and the club was crowded, Spanish Rock night. The music, mostly Spanish, was booming, feeling every beat in my chest. One of the few whettos in the club, I felt out of place, but dancing with Emily made all of my insecurities worth it. Emily and I danced and talked all night long. For the first time since I had gone undercover, I actually began to have fun and lose myself. Emily's body effortlessly moved in ways I had never seen a woman's body move before. Every movement was seductive, but innocent.

As the night progressed, Emily and I became one and the guilt I had been feeling about Liz was no longer on my mind. I told Emily about my broken past, just like the training unit had taught me, and they were right, she believed everything I told her. Lie after lie: I told her that my parents had left me when I was young and how my grandmother had raised me, and how my dad had been killed in Vietnam and my real mom was a heroin addict. All of this Emily took in, pulling on her heart strings, drawing her closer to me. Emily sympathized with me, praised me, and marveled at how well I was able to handle my past experiences… and I knew she was mine, just like Sam had told me would happen.

As we were dancing a guy bumped into Emily, startling her. I saw him wink at her as she dismissed his behavior. As the song continued, so did the bumping, but now it became purposeful, and I could tell the guy was showing off in front of his friends. The anger inside me began to build and I knew my pride was taking over my rationality, just as Sam had warned me. The tiger that lived inside me and which had caused me much grief growing up began to waken. I knew if this guy was successful in waking up the tiger that lay deep inside me, it would end badly. So I controlled my emotions and simply switched places with Emily, blocking her from the guy.

Finally, I grabbed Emily's hand and pulled her off the dance floor. "Em, let's go get a drink," I yelled.

Emily nodded her head in agreement as we left the dance floor and walked towards the bar. Two seats opened up at the bar, and we sat down and ordered a couple of drinks and carried on our conversation. As I took a drink, I saw the guy from the dance floor approaching me from my left, but I didn't make eye contact with him. He walked past me and stood next to Emily on her right side. He slid a business card with his phone number written on it across the table. I just shook my head as he walked away, saying nothing.

During the next song, I noticed the guy maneuvering his way around the crowd to get next to Emily again, but she was too immersed in the music to notice him. Then she suddenly jumped forward into my arms, looking back, this time in sheer anger at the guy.

"That guy just grabbed my ass!" she yelled. "Can we leave, Steven?" she asked.

Realizing what he'd just done, I instinctively moved towards him…

"What's up, whetto? What you gunna do, motherfucker?" he said with a smirk on his face.

Emily stood in between us with her hands on my chest pushing me backwards…

"Steven, no! Let's just go," she pleaded, pushing me backwards.

A succession of thoughts ran through my head: *What do I do? I could get kicked out of the program if I get into a bar fight. I'm an undercover cop. Let it go, Mac. There is a far bigger picture here than my date getting her ass grabbed in a club.* I turned and we started to leave the club, then I stopped after a few steps. It was too late… The tiger woke up when I pictured the smirk on this guy's face and his sheer disrespect of Emily and me.

My father had raised me to stand up for what I believed was right; it was ingrained in me and I couldn't stop it. Flashing in my head from years of martial arts training was my sensei's voice: "When we are confronted… There are no rules; you don't fight fair; you strike first, you strike hard, you don't stop until it's done," he'd always lectured us.

I pushed Emily aside and turned to find the guy. I saw him about fifteen feet in front of me, with his friends nearby.

"Dom, Dom, Dom," I heard Emily yelling.

Without warning, just as I came within striking distance of that smirk, I kicked him square in the balls with everything I had. His torso fell forward just as I knew it would, and I grabbed his hair to keep his head from falling too far, and kneed him in the face. His nose shattered on impact and he fell to the floor as I ducked one punch from my left. Rising back up, I struck one of his friends in the face, sending him backwards over a railing as the crowd began to scatter. One of his friends clipped me, cutting my face and the familiar salty taste of blood entered my mouth. I threw an elbow as another of his friends came at me, striking him on the side of his face... Before I knew it, I was being bear-hugged from behind, lifted off my feet and slammed onto the ground.

"Steven, what the fuck bro, it's Dom... Bro, it's Dom, Steven, it's Dom. Chill the fuck out!" Dom was yelling in my right ear as he continued to hold me on the ground; I sensed he was covering me from being kicked.

Dom and another bouncer lifted me to my feet and escorted me out the back door of the club; my face was bleeding slightly, but I could tell the cut wasn't bad. Dom, six-foot-four and two-hundred-twenty-five pounds of muscle, stood there asking me, "What happened, bro?"

"I'm sorry, Dom. I didn't mean to disrespect you in your club," I tried to explain. I told him the story and I apologized again for getting into a fight in his club.

I saw a red light coming down the back alley at a high rate of speed as the familiar sound of a siren chirp grew louder. Surprisingly I wasn't scared… I guess because another one of my father's life lessons was "There are consequences for everything in life, but sometimes they are worth it, son." I saw two uniformed officers talking to the club manager and a couple of guys I assumed were bouncers; the manager then pointed at me and I saw the officers acknowledge him, turn and start walking towards my direction.

"What's your name buddy?" one officer asked me.

"Steven, sir," I responded.

"Steven, I need you to stand up and put your hands on top of your head. Do you understand me?" he told me with command presence.

"Yes sir," I responded, as I stood up, placing my hands on top of my head and turning away from him.

"I see you know the routine… how many times have you been arrested before?" he asked.

"I've never been arrested before, sir," I answered.

The officer firmly secured my hands, locking my fingers together, causing slight pain in my hands, and searched me for weapons. Next thing I knew I was handcuffed and placed in the back of the patrol car. His handcuffing technique was flawless. I was very impressed… it was quick and I never felt like he lost control of my hands during any portion of the process. The handcuffs were positioned in the right direction on my wrists and he had double-locked them, preventing them from getting tighter when I sat down. I remember sitting in the back of the patrol car thinking, *Man, there is no room back here and it smells.*

I saw Emily talking to the other officer. Her mascara was running down her face. "Steven, are you okay? Are you hurt?" she called out to me as the officer was trying to console her. "Officer, please let him go, he didn't do anything wrong. That guy assaulted me!" Em pleaded with the officer. A common mistake most civilians make is not knowing the definition of assault. "Officer, officer, please don't do this. I'm telling you, he was just protecting me from that guy. That guy assaulted me! I want to press charges. Officer, I want to press charges!" She continued to plead with the officer as she went to battle for my freedom. I'm not going to lie, it was one of the weirdest moments of my life. There I was, an undercover police officer about ready to get arrested for getting into a bar fight for protecting my girlfriend, who really wasn't my girlfriend and didn't even know my real name… WTH!

Em's persistence paid off and the officer allowed her to talk to me through the window of the patrol car.

"Don't worry, Em, I'm all right," I told her.

"You're bleeding! Oh my gosh, officer, he's bleeding!" Em began to cry again.

"Em, it's just a scratch. I promise," I tried to console her.

"Officer, do you mind if I give her my car keys so she can get home? They're in my left front," I said.

"Standby, but I'll make sure she gets home," the officer responded.

I looked through the caged window and saw one officer talking to Dom as the other officer was running my name for warrants. I heard my name come back clean over the radio as the officer acknowledged the operator and started walking over to the patrol car.

"Alright, Steven, here's the deal. Witnesses said that the other guy is the one that started the fight and that you were just protecting yourself and your girlfriend. Do you want to press charges?" the officer asked me.

"No sir, I do not," I responded quickly.

"Okay, that's your choice. He's got a warrant so we are going to arrest him on that anyway. Do you want the medic to take a look at that cut?"

"No sir… I'll get it taken care of," I said, just wanting to get out of there.

"Okay, your choice again. I'm going to get you out of there, but I need you to sign this saying you are refusing medical treatment. Do you understand?"

"Yes sir, I do," I responded again, hoping to hurry the process along.

The officer let me out of the car and uncuffed me and I went right to where Emily was standing.

"Steven, why did you do that? You could have gotten in serious trouble," she said, her emotions changing to what I sensed was a bit of anger, instead of the gratitude I'd been expecting.

"I'm sorry Em," I said and paused, before saying it again. "I'm sorry." I didn't know what else to say to her. I wanted to tell her the whole truth. I wanted her to know Drew, not Steven. I felt bad for lying to her, but I guess that was my job. As I drove her back to her apartment, there was a battle going on inside me because I really wanted to tell her the truth; a moment of weakness and vulnerability. We didn't talk and when we arrived in front of her apartment and I turned off the engine, the silence got heavy.

"Steven, I thought you were different, but you're not," she said, refusing to make eye contact with me. "You are just a white version of every other guy I've dated from the neighborhood... I can't do this again. I'm not going to do this again. I promised myself, I was not going to do this." Her eyes began to well up.

I didn't answer. I just stared off into space, not wanting to look at her face and fall prey to those innocent eyes.

"Don't you have anything to say to me?" she asked, this time with a bit of anger in her voice.

"Em, I can't…" I responded, offering no rebuttal or explanation because I was honestly at a loss for words and I didn't want to lie to her, but I had no truth to offer.

"Why not?! Steven, talk to me!" Em said as she wiped at her tears. "I thought you were different, but you're not. Don't call me. Bye, Steven!" She opened my car door, and never looked back.

90-Day Review

"There is an Ocean of Silence Between Us

And I'm Drowning in it…"

Ranata Suziki

Beep... beep... beep... "920-2222."

"What are you, some sort of drug deal Whocco?" Oz asked me as he helped me ring out a customer.

"No, but maybe I should be. Do you think a white boy could sell drugs around here?" I said with a laugh as I handed the bag to the customer.

"You know, you probably shouldn't be talking about selling drugs around customers. I'm going to report you to your manager," a customer said in disgust, grabbing her bag.

"Yo, Whocco! That shit was funny, bro! She was pissed. It's always the white people that get pissed over stupid shit." Oz shook his head. "Yo, Whocco... Why are your people so uptight? You know, I was fucking this white chick one time and she wouldn't let me turn the lights on? What's up with that, bro? Is that a white thing?" Oz continued his rant as I walked away to call JT.

"Oz, cover me, bro, I'll be right back," I said.

"I got you cuz," Oz said, as I just shook my head because he had so many names for me. I didn't think he actually knew my real name – or my real fake name, I should say. I walked across the street to a local Hispanic grocery store where there was a rather clean bank of pay

204

phones. I entered my calling card number; I'd finally evolved from a pocket full of quarters to a pre-paid calling card.

"JT's barber shop," JT answered. *You know, maybe Oz is right*, I thought to myself. *These Mexicans know what's up.*

"JT, what's up? Everything okay?" I asked.

"Sure is, Junior. Meet me at Location No. 2 tomorrow at 8," he said as he continued to laugh at his own joke.

Location No. 2 was one of three pre-designated meet locations and I hadn't been there since early on in my training. The location was a medium-size dog park that had a fenced area for dogs and bench table seating around the outer perimeter. What made this location special was that the back side of the park looked wooded, which was very rare in a large metropolitan area with no exit. Just beyond the wooded tree-line was a small dirt bike path that breached the tall oaks. It was very deceiving and most of the park attendees had no idea it even existed. Following the path, it opened up to a series of brick walls, where I could only imagine had once stood a magnificent home. Your options then varied as you entered the maze of bricks… Choose left and you ended up in the alleyway behind a favorite neighborhood liquor store; the employees took regular breaks sitting on an old couch that had been abandoned in the alleyway. Choose right, follow the bike path and your destiny would be a Tam's No. 9 restaurant, about three hundred yards to the east. Choose to stay, and there was plenty of cover, but there wasn't much concealment beyond the bricks.

"Okay, will do. What's up?" I asked.

"Relax, all is good, Junior. It's your 90-day review and I have some mail for you. See you tomorrow at 0800." JT hung up the phone without saying goodbye and before I could ask him if I really had a 90-day review.

As I walked back into the store, "Steven, dial 300," broadcast over the loudspeakers, but I didn't realize that the "Steven" was really me. I continued to walk back to the electronics department where I had been assigned for the day. Oz looked swamped with customers as I hurried back to help him. "Yo, Whocco. What did they say?" he asked.

"What did who say?" I replied as my heart began to race and my hands started to sweat. I immediately thought my cover was blown, a constant concern, but Oz was just concerned about my phone call.

"What you mean, foo? What did Dan say?" Oz looked at me, eager for my response.

"Steven, DIAL 300," the voice bellowed throughout the store again.

I looked up at the ceiling where the sound was bellowing from, now realizing that they were talking about me. I quickly entered the electronics department, passing through the swinging door and grabbing the red phone there.

"Crazy Whocco. You didn't call him, foo. The man sounds pissed!" Oz chuckled, shaking his head as he continued to try and make a dent in a long line of frustrated customers waiting to pay for their items.

I dialed 300 and the store manager Dan – or as Oz referred to him, *The Man* – ordered me upstairs to see him in his office. I found a humorous parody in Oz's name for the store manager; JT had referred to the Chief of Police the same way; I guess everyone has their form of *The Man.*

Dan (The Man) – 5'8, 190 lbs, pudgy, mid-forties, shockingly bilingual because you wouldn't guess it based on his profile; he always had on a wrinkled dress shirt, typically white, and always short-sleeved. Glasses, black frames that often sat on the bridge of his nose. Walked with a distinct gait, his right foot dragging behind with a slight hint of pigeon toe. Hair balding with the typical denial; a comb-over from left to right.

"Steve, come on in. Take a seat," Dan said as he peered over his glasses. I took a seat... His office was typical sized. One side was covered with golf memorabilia, directly behind his desk were three plaques for store manager awards, and another wall had a book credenza with photos of his family, and a simple Bible verse framed in a red cherry oak frame with a signature that I couldn't read. As I took a seat, I assessed the situation: Dan was leaning back in his chair and his foot was draped over the corner of his desk, his face appeared relaxed, his eyes widened when I entered the room, his right hand was twirling a pencil with an occasional tap on his desk. Confused, I sat down.

"Steve, or is it Steven?" Dan asked as he removed his foot from the desk and sat up in his chair.

"Either one is good, sir," I responded. So far, I was not impressed.

"Okay, great. Hey Steve, we had a complaint... the guest said you were talking about selling drugs? I'm sure it wasn't you because you don't seem like the drug dealer type. It was Oswaldo, wasn't it?" Dan dropped his leg onto the ground and sat up in his chair, making a loud creaking sound as he looked for confirmation. "It's okay, you can tell me. I won't say anything… This is just between you and me. These fucking bangers selling shit in my store and he's probably stealing me blind too. My losses are going through the roof!" Dan's eyebrows pinched inward, his eyes fixated, and he stopped twirling the pencil. "Was it him?" he asked me again, now sitting erect in his chair.

"No sir… I think that lady misunderstood, because we weren't talking about drug dealing. Oz was just helping me out because I was swamped. I don't think Oz messes around with any drugs," I said.

Dan seemed shocked by my response and continued to question me. "Are you sure? I've cleaned this store up and he's one of the last bangers and I can't get rid of him," Dan rambled and I could tell he regretted saying the last sentence out loud.

"Sir, is that course Pebble Beach?" I asked, trying to deflect.

"It is! Steve, you golf?" Dan faced his body towards the picture and for the next fifteen minutes talked about all of the golf pictures he had displayed in his office. I left shortly thereafter and didn't face any disciplinary action.

The next day, I traveled to meet JT at location No. 2. I left early to make sure to follow my Op Sec procedures prior to my arrival. I saw

JT and Jack waiting at the table located at the south of the park so I made my approach from the west. I would have preferred to sit at the east table because the slight breeze coming out of the east would have masked the smell of dog feces; I made the suggestion to JT and Jack to move tables but they seemed bothered by my suggestion and motioned me to sit down.

I had been feeling a little apprehensive about the meeting, but I really didn't know why. Deep down inside, I think I was hoping to see Sam since she had made me feel more at ease, but I wasn't that lucky today. I wondered why JT had brought *Jack Ass* – the self-coined name I'd given him, which was well deserved. JT had to know I really didn't care that much for Jack Ass and I was certain the feeling was mutual. A definite match of dislikes would have been a generous label.

As I walked up to meet them, Jack Ass was on his phone and gave me a *Metro Nod* as my acknowledgement, then turned his back to me. JT seemed truly happy to see me and for the first time I didn't feel like he was out to get me or catch me. We exchanged niceties and the standard general small talk. It was short, because JT wasn't supposed to ask me any questions about which group I was investigating or anything about my cover life. My anxiety subsided as JT made me laugh, telling me the same three jokes that I honestly couldn't tell if he remembered telling me before on several occasions, but it felt good to laugh and I felt a peacefulness for the first time since I'd gone *under the sheets*, as they called it.

"Hey, kid, do you want your mail first or do you want to do our admin crap first? I hate this admin bullshit. Hey Jack, why do we have to do this shit for birds?" JT started on a slight rant.

"Let's do your stuff first," I requested.

"Okay, kid, here are some training orders I need you to sign and some Police Officer Standards stuff I have to check you off on. The rest of this stuff is your probationary paperwork. Oh, congratulations, you just made probation... You have officially been a cop for eighteen months and the city can't get rid of you now, kid." JT started to laugh. "Welcome to Civil Service Protection."

After eighteen months, if an officer made probation, they were automatically promoted to the next rank, with a standard 5% pay raise, but more importantly, the officer now had Civil Service Protection: their career was locked. In my case, I'd completed the police academy, only spent four months in the field, five months in UC training and now three months as a UC and boom, I was off probation. I was shocked! My thoughts turned towards my classmates – I wondered how they were doing. Had everyone else made probation? Were they going to throw a party like past traditions?

"Hey JT... How does it work? I mean what if my classmates are looking for me to invite me to a party? What do they think happened to me?" I asked.

"Most of the time they only look for you at the end of probation, then they forget about you, kid," JT told it to me straight.

"And what will they find, if they look?"

"You don't exist anymore on the books, kid. We told you that." JT seemed bothered by what he considered a rudimentary question.

"I know, but what does it actually show?" I continued, undeterred by his frustration.

"It shows you didn't make probation, but it doesn't give a reason."

Over the next hour, JT went over all the administrative and training paperwork required by the Department or the state to maintain my police officer status. Next, he went over my financials, which was interesting. A secret checking account had been set up at the Police Credit Union, just using a number – 1503 – instead of my name, and my normal police salary was being transferred into the account twice a month. I had no access to the account, however. Strange when I look back on it… youth and love are always blind, I guess. JT handed me the checking account statement, displaying my beginning balance and my ending balance, $10,230, which I initialed in acknowledgement. I remember looking at that first bank statement with a balance of over $10K in three months… Not too bad, I thought, doing a quick calculation in my head to see how long it would take me to save my goal of a hundred-thousand.

JT handed me a large manila envelope stuffed with what I assumed was my mail – my first connection to Mac's life since going under the sheets. *'1503'* had been written across the length of the envelope in large blue inked letters. The handwriting appeared to be that of a left-handed woman, based on the slant and the curve of the numbers. Was Sam left-handed or was there another female that I hadn't seen in SAU? Not knowing if Sam was left-handed made an impression on me, since I was supposed to be a trained professional observer.

I quickly shuffled through the stuffed envelope of mail and saw two letters from Liz which were easily recognizable from the imprint of her lips across the seal. I grabbed them, setting the rest of the mail down on the picnic table.

"Ah, I would grab that one too," JT said with a sleazy tone, but I didn't engage. Feeling like a convict with two guards overseeing my every movement, I took my mail and walked over to the eastside table where I'd originally wanted to sit. My hands began to sweat and my heart began to race with excitement as I started to read her words. I imagined her face and smile as I read her words of sheer sadness. Liz was beyond devastated and was having a hard time dealing with our situation. On closer inspection of the letter, I saw the marks on the paper where her tears must have fallen. The letter finished with loving thoughts, but a ton of guilt overcame me as I quickly began to doubt my decision to choose this life over a girl I loved. Was I being selfish?

I opened Liz's second letter... *'For Your Eyes Only'* had been written across a carefully folded piece of white lined school paper. As I opened it, there it was, a picture of her lying in her bed dressed in a sexy outfit I didn't recognize. An immediate smile came across my face. The caption read: 'I Got This for You!' I shook my head and continued to stare at her picture with some resolve that she was okay.

After finishing going through all my mail and paying a few remaining bills that Mac had, I felt a new energy. Liz and the rest of my friends and family had all given me overwhelming support, albeit with obvious concern. I felt loved and not alone anymore…

"You all done?" JT asked me as I sat down at his table.

"I think so… Is there anything else we need to do?" I asked.

"Nope… We're good, except for one thing." JT's tone changed ever so slightly.

"What's that?"

"I'm sorry… but you can't keep the picture." His is gaze fixed on mine.

I paused, processing what JT was saying, but still not answering him, knowing that keeping Liz's photo would be considered a crossover, which is never safe.

"You should know that, Mac!" Jack chimed in from across the table.

True, as you should know not to call me Mac, my inner voice answered, a voice I had a history of failing to control.

I pulled out Liz's picture, concealing it from these two vultures as I placed it back into the envelope.

"Here's the way this works. Items you want to keep you put in this bag and we will give it all back to you when you get out. All of the other items you don't want put in this bag and we'll shred them," JT explained.

I nodded in acknowledgement as I placed all of my letters into the saved bag. We shook hands and went to say our goodbyes.

"Wait, you haven't heard the best part yet of your ninety-day review," JT boasted.

"Yeah, what's that?" I answered, expecting a smart-ass response.

"You've earned your first conjugal visit back home – that's if you want one?" JT started to smile.

"What do you mean? I asked.

"It's been three months and you get a few days off to do whatever it is as Mac. You can go see your buddies, your girl, or your family. Just let your handlers know when and we'll make it happen, but remember you can't tell them anything about who you are or what you've been doing." JT's face straightened as he responded.

An uncontrolled smile appeared across my face as I said quickly, "I would like to see Liz as soon as possible."

"I figured you would say that. We'll contact her and take care of all of the arrangements. Here's what's going to happen…"

In my excitement, I interrupted JT mid-sentence. "How will this work?"

"We'll tell you where to meet us and we'll exchange IDs and give you back Mac's stuff, but you won't have your police identification and you can't carry a gun because remember, there is no record of you as a police officer. She is going to ask you a ton of questions and you are going to want to tell her, but don't do it, for her safety and yours… I'll be in touch with you in a couple of days." JT began to get up.

"Thank you, JT, I really appreciate it," I told him as we shook hands.

Turning and purposely not shaking my hand, Jack said under his breath, "Don't worry, *Steven,* I won't look at your little girlfriend's photo."

"Jack," said JT. "Shut the fuck up!"

I pondered all the way back to my apartment why some people were just Adam Henrys, the term police use to refer to Ass Holes. Their lives seem so miserable… But what perplexed me the most was why I was so bothered that Jack didn't like me.

217

A few days later, JT and I spoke and he told me to meet him at a storage facility in the Valley. When I pulled up, the gate automatically opened but I didn't see who or know why it opened for me. I looked down at my pager and read the storage unit number, 552G, as I navigated the multi-floor storage facility. As I rounded the corner on the fifth floor, I saw Sam standing outside a storage unit motioning for me. Long black boots hugging her legs, stopping just above her calves, black skirt, with a sweater hiding her breasts, her hair braided in a ponytail but resting off to the right side.

Sam turned and opened the roller door of the storage unit, motioning for me to park inside, and greeting me with a big smile as I parked. Then she stepped inside and shut the roll-up door behind her, and the storage unit darkened. I heard her lock the door from the inside as she turned on a light located at the back of the otherwise empty storage unit.

"Steven, how are you?" she asked as I got out of my car.

"I'm well, how are you?" I never really knew how to respond to this girl, but it was good to see her.

"You look different," she said, as I felt her give me a once over with her eyes. "It must be the beard or the long hair," she added as she gave me a gentle but longer than normal hug. I felt her fingers run through the back of my hair, which was now almost long enough to put in a ponytail. Her familiar scent was consuming and flustered me slightly.

"How are you?" I asked her.

"I'm good," she said, then shifted her tone to all business. "So, Steven, just leave everything in here. Don't take anything with you that will be a crossover. Don't worry, it will be safe here."

"Sounds good," I said as I removed all of Steven's stuff and placed it in my vehicle.

"Just leave your keys inside, but obviously don't lock it. Here you go… And Hocus Pocus! You are now back to Mac! Hi Mac, my name is Lisa. Nice to meet you." Sam extended her hand.

"Your real name is Lisa?"

"No, silly, I was just messing with you." Sam looked up towards the cold concrete ceiling. "Shoot… Hey, we have to go – that's your ride! Follow me." Sam walked towards the corner of the storage unit where I saw a metal ladder leading up to an opening in the ceiling.

"Sam, where are we going? What is that?"

"Just follow me and make sure you have everything," she said as she started to climb the ladder in her skirt and knee-high boots. I watched, looking upwards at Sam's exposed underskirt, still not quite understanding what was going on.

Sam pushed the hatch open as I began to climb the ladder after her, entering what looked like a small electrical or utility room. The room, full of dust and cobwebs, had a musty smell to it. I heard what sounded distinctly like a helicopter.

"Mac, here they come. When they land the bird, remember, don't go near the tail. Stay even with the door on approach from the front. When you get inside, put on your headset and that will give you comms with the pilot," Sam said as the dust started to stir in the room from the force of the rotor wind coming through the cracks of the door.

"Sam, is that a helicopter?" I yelled to overcome the rotor noise.

"No, it's a train silly," she yelled back; I smiled, realizing the ignorance of my question, and turned to board the bird.

"Wait, Steven… I'm not supposed to tell you, but when you get back, they are going to assign you," she told me, realizing immediately she shouldn't have.

"Who's my target?" I asked her.

"KKK."

The rooftop door opened and the co-pilot motioned for me to approach.

The helicopter was matte black with no markings and I didn't recognize it as one of our law enforcement helicopters. The pilot and co-pilot were both dressed in olive green flight suits, patchless, both wearing helmets with visors concealing their identities. As I sat down in the bird, I was handed a headset.

"Welcome, sir. We have a short flight over to Bracket where you will meet your party," I heard over my headset.

I tried respond, but didn't hear my voice broadcast.

"Sir, you have to put the microphone closer to your mouth, then we can hear you."

I moved the mic closer to my mouth.

"Bird3 to Tower, come in," I heard the pilot say over the air.

"Tower to Bird3, go ahead, sir," a robotic, steady but seemingly experienced voice answered.

"Roger, Tower, Bird3 starting King Unit's transport out of the Northwest, flight time and route filed, mark time now," the pilot said, as I felt the bird lift off, hovering approximately ten feet off the ground as the front of the bird began to turn to the east, rising slightly. The nose dipped as we took off, weaving and climbing above the high-rise office buildings.

"Roger, Bird3, you are clear, safe travels to you and the King Unit's transport, good day," the steely voice announced.

As we flew off overlooking the city, I couldn't help but have a moment of pause, still not fully understanding what I had signed up for with this program, but feeling this was really cool and special. Every turn seemed to have another mystery that was never really explained very well and you had to be able to adapt to anything on a moment's notice; just roll with the punches with very little information. Today's adventure had seemed so simple when I'd gotten out of bed that morning, but now, here I was flying in a helicopter for the first time in my life, after hiding my car in some secret squirrel storage building, crawling through a roof hatch to board a helicopter... and all of this just to see my girlfriend who had no idea what I was doing or where I was staying... *Really?* I chuckled to myself, as I admired the views of the city for the next twenty minutes.

"Sir, we are going to be Code 6," the co-pilot announces over the air. "Please stay in the bird until I open the door for you. It's been our pleasure, sir… Bird3 to Tower, King Unit transport complete, mark time. Over."

I nodded to the pilots to show my admiration and appreciation for the experience as I climbed out of the bird. The co-pilot handed me my bag from a rear compartment and motioned me to walk towards a building approximately fifty yards away, where I saw David waiting for me just outside a brown metal door. I looked back as the helicopter began to hover, rising gradually, then taking a hard bank to the west out of my sight as the rotor washes blew across my body.

"Hey Mac, great to see you again. Everything okay with you?" David asked.

"Yeah, I'm good, David, thanks," I said as we walked inside the building, which was nondescript, similar to an office building.

"Mac, here are the keys to a car. It's the tan Camry parked outside. The plates are cold so don't worry. There's a package inside the car with your destination and everything you need. It's a house on the coast and it's nice. When you get there, give Liz a call and have her come up. It's about a three-hour drive for her so you can call her now if you like so she can get on the road. Sorry, Mac, but I need you to still check in with me just once in the morning and once in the evening, but all you have to do is page me. Do you have any questions?"

"What about when I come back? How does that work?" I asked.

"Just call me the night before and I'll walk you through it. Don't sweat it, just have fun with your girl. Talk to you in a couple of days," David said as he walked away.

I felt like I'd just been released from prison. It was the little things that I was most excited about, I guess: making a phone call from my house, having a face-to-face conversation with someone who actually knew the real me, not having to constantly lie, compartmentalizing the truth.

The house, I later found out, was owned by Claire and her husband. It was their vacation home and it was perfect. A small cottage, immaculately kept, secluded, with great attention to detail, overlooking the ocean. Everything was just as David had said it would be and actually there was a nice welcoming package for us with a hand-written note reading, *Mac, here are a few of your favorites. Enjoy your time and thank you for your dedication.* The wicker basket contained champagne, cheese, crackers, olives, and my favorite candy: sweet tarts – the hard kind that came in a package of three, unlike the gooey ones they sell today; to this day I still wonder how whoever was responsible for the basket knew that was my favorite candy.

A small deck out back had a secured perimeter of mature trees on sides two and four, with side three open to a magnificent view of the Pacific Ocean. Plopped in the middle of the deck was a hot tub, a couple of lounge chairs, and a hammock, all calling my name.

A few hours after I arrived, I saw Liz's jeep turn up the driveway and I rushed outside to see her. My heart began to race as her Jeep drew closer. Liza's hair was blowing in the wind as she had the Jeep's top and doors off, and was driving at a much faster speed than she should be. Her smile was huge. She was wearing mirrored sunglasses and a tank top. I saw her hand extend up through the top of the Jeep, waving at me as I waited for her at the end of the driveway.

"Oh my gosh, Mac, look at you! Your hair, a beard," she shouted as she ran and jumped into my arms. Her familiar smell was comforting.

"I know it's long, huh? I hate it but I'm getting used to it," I said as we continued to embrace. I can't describe the feeling but I didn't want to let go of her. I felt safe, loved and not alone.

"It's curly… I never knew you had curly hair! Babe! Your baby face is gone," she continued, staring at me as I showed her around the house.

"Hey, let me get the groceries out of my Jeep," she said, stopping the tour short.

"Groceries?" I inquired.

"Yup, I figured you could use a home-cooked meal because God only knows that you can't cook, babe." She laughed and I nodded in acknowledgement. "Besides, my mother always told me the way to a man's heart is through his stomach and if that doesn't work, I have gifts," she continued as we grabbed the groceries, and I suddenly realized that after I'd switched identities I'd forgotten to stop and get a gift for her.

"Liz…" I paused, not quite sure what to say, but I knew I wanted to say something.

Liz stopped unloading the groceries and looked at me. We locked eyes.

"Thank you for coming," I said.

She just smiled and went about her task.

"No, Liz… really, thank you for coming." My voice cracked and emotions that I couldn't control overcame me as I fought back tears.

"Ahh, Mac," she said as she walked over to embrace me. "Are you okay?" she whispered in my ear as we embraced.

I didn't respond, trying not to cry in front of her.

"Babe, it's okay. I'm here. We're together. I love you…"

I still didn't answer her, trying to put the brakes on my potential breakdown and fears.

"Look at me, Mr. MacGregor! Knock it off. We are going to get through this, you hear me? Just hurry up and do whatever you are doing and get back to me!" Liz was in full Latina mode and I loved it.

We spent the next few days together rekindling our bond, laughing, joking, hiking, eating ice cream, walking on the beach and of course sipping champagne for the first time in my life. I must say it's the one thing the French can do on their own is make a great champagne…

Liz and I got up early and went for our regular hike in the morning knowing that we only had one morning left before I had to go back under the sheets. The waves were temperamental, the tops disappearing like a David Copperfield special. We sat on a flat rock overlooking the cliff, watching each set of waves crash against the shore. Violent, humbling…

As we started to walk back to the house Liz said, "Mac, I don't want to leave. Can you call your people and ask to stay a few more days? I'll call in sick."

"Call my people?" I started to laugh. "I wish we could. But the longer I stay here with you, the longer it will take for me to get back to you." For once a rational thought had entered my head. As we approached the house, I saw a plain wrap car parked in the driveway. I knew it was a police vehicle but didn't recognize it.

"Damn it! They said they wouldn't bother me and all I had to do was check in, which I did!" I said, quickening my pace.

"What, Mac? What is it? Who is it?" Liz could now also see the car parked on the side of the house.

"I don't know… Man, I can't catch a break with these guys," I said in frustration. "Hey, babe, you don't have to say shit to these guys. Don't say shit to these guys if they want to interview you," I said in a harsh tone.

"Interview me? What's going on, Mac? I'm scared." Liz slowed her pace as we started down the long gravel driveway.

"I'm sorry, babe. I didn't mean to scare you. It's okay. I'm just pissed, that's all. This is supposed to be our time and these motherfuckers won't leave me alone."

A man I didn't recognize got out of the plain wrap. Six foot two, approximately twenty-eight years old, dark hair thinning on top where sunglasses once rested across his head. Cop eyes, cop walk, cop mannerisms. This guy was a poster boy for the thin blue line. Gun, .45-caliber Smith & Wesson, proudly displayed on his left hip next to his police badge, a single magazine on his right hip, next to a small container of OC spray, raid jacket tucked in neatly, perfect creases along the sleeves. His face was serious but he appeared nervous. As we approached, he said, "Mac, Liz, nice to meet you, ma'am" and extended his hand. "My name is Mick, truly sorry to bother you both and I'm sorry we had to meet this way but Albert sent me…"

I set my anger aside because Mick actually seemed genuine and sincere.

"Mac, may I speak with you in private please?" he asked.

"Sure. Babe, just go inside – I'll be in there in a minute. Everything's okay, babe. I promise. I'll be right in."

"Hey, Mac… sorry again, bro, but Albert's been trying to get ahold of you. Do you have your pager?" Mick asked me.

"Fuck him! They told me this is my time and I only needed to check in once a day which I have been doing. These guys just like to fuck with me. Unbelievable!" My anger was now exploding.

"Mac, Mac, Mac …" Mick stopped my rant.

"What?"

"Hey, I get it man, and I'm sorry we had to meet this way, but have you watched the news lately?" Mick asked.

"No, what happened?"

"A truck bomb exploded out in front of the Federal Building in Oklahoma City yesterday morning and it killed a bunch of people, man, including kids."

"Oh wow. I didn't know. But what does that have to do with us? Are they from California?"

"An up and coming group we are told is responsible for the bombing. They call themselves militias or sovereign citizens and we don't know shit about them, Mac," Mick said, staring at me.

I realized what he was saying.

"Mac, these groups will fall into our shop, under white power. This came down from the Chief last night and Mac I mean *the Chief*. You're the only guy we have who has a chance to infiltrate these motherfuckers. It's on you, bro."

"Damn, are you serious? What's your name again?"

"Mick, Mick is my name. I'm Irish! What can I say?" He cracked a smile. "Hey listen, there's a militia meeting tonight and the Chief wants you there. That's why I'm here."

"The meeting is tonight?"

"Unfortunately, yes, and we have to go because you have to be briefed before the meeting."

"Okay, and where's the meeting?"

"Bakersfield."

"Bakersfield? That's fucking far. I'll never make that," I said.

"Don't worry. There's a bird inbound right now to pick you up and fly you back to Steven's car. Sam will meet you at the LZ and do the exchange. Don't worry about this car, I'll take care of everything, but Liz has to go."

When I walked back inside the house Liz was sitting on the patio deck staring out at the ocean, holding my pager in her hand. "Someone paged you six times, Mac. What is going on? What is so urgent? I know something happened. You don't have to be a cop to see it on that guy's face and his hands were sweaty just like how yours get when you're nervous. I know – you can't tell me. I know the drill." She sounded defeated. She stood up and went to gather her things.

Mick was standing outside, looking at his military-style watch nervously, talking into a hand-held radio occasionally, but we couldn't hear the dialogue from inside. Liz and I gathered our things and made sure the house was in order. "Mac, can we say goodbye here? I just feel weird saying goodbye in front of him. I know, silly, right?"

"No, babe. Not at all. Whatever you want." I felt bad and already missed her.

"I love you, Mr. MacGregor! You come back to me, you hear?" Liz gave me a longer than normal hug and a kiss on the cheek. I remember the hug… it was disconnected, or maybe defeated is a better word. I helped her load her stuff into her Jeep and we said goodbye one last time before she headed back home down the long gravel driveway. The mood was somber and I couldn't help but think that I might have just lost her.

Shortly after Liz left, I heard the bird inbound. I knew it was close but couldn't see it at first. Then I saw Mick pop smoke in a nearby parking lot he'd cordoned off. The smoke was purple, filling the air quickly, signaling to the bird where to land. As the bird landed, what was once extraordinary now seemed to be routine as I boarded the bird from the rear, taking my seat, this time placing the mic from my headset nearer my mouth so the pilots could hear me. The bird performed a hot landing, the rotors never stopping, and took off as quickly as it had landed. A short hover, the nose of the bird dipped, forward thrust, and away we went, hugging the California coastline towards the city. We passed over what I was certain was Liz's Jeep along the four-lane coast highway.

As I flew back to the city, I maintained radio silence, not because of protocol, more because I really didn't have anything to say. Not only had my assignment changed, but I now knew what Lieutenant Kelly had spoken of: my life just changed forever. I understood the gravity of the situation and understood these final minutes cruising along the most beautiful coastline in the country were most likely my last moments of peace. My stomach would sink on occasion throughout the flight, but I wasn't sure if it was due to turbulence or the sinking feeling coming over

me that I might not make it out of this new assignment alive.

Look for . . .

Going it Alone

LAPD's Last Operative

Volume No. 2